Susan Janet Roach was born in Lancashire on 3rd November, 1950. She attended elementary school in Burnley and later attended grammar/boarding school in Yorkshire in the 1960s.

On leaving school she joined the Lancashire Constabulary and later transferred to London's Metropolitan Police until the end of her thirty years' service. She was employed as a detective constable for most of her service with the Metropolitan, serving in the South London area.

Now retired, she resides in Northern Ireland and when not writing enjoys long seaside walks with her two black Labradors, Jack and Laddie.

This book is dedicated to my new family and to the innocent people of Northern Ireland that 'Wee Geordie' fought for.

S. J. Roach

OUR WEE GEORDIE

AUSTIN MACAULEY
PUBLISHERS LTD.

A CIP catalogue record for this title is available from the British Library.

ISBN 9781786124418 (Paperback)
ISBN 9781786124425 (Hardback)
ISBN 9781786124432 (EBook)

www.austinmacauley.com

First Published (2016)
Austin Macauley Publishers Ltd.
25 Canada Square
Canary Wharf
London
E14 5LQ

Acknowledgments

Dr John Hamill who was an enormous help to me with all his advice, and Georgina Brown who helped me with the editing in the early years of writing. Sincere thanks to you both.

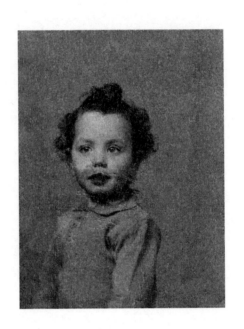

Chapter One

The Ladies' Hairdresser

'There's no bloody ladies' hairdresser coming to live in this house.' Those were the words of my brother Dickie; he was a good deal older than me – in fact he was twelve years older and the most outspoken member of our family. He was on home leave from the Merchant Navy; it was good to see him and for us all to be sitting round the table having our meals together.

I was fifteen and was working for a company called Stevenson and Turner, in Belfast, as their message boy. One Friday night I'd told Mr Charlie McMahon that I was handing in my notice as I was going to be a ladies' hairdresser. Mr McMahon was a dapper little man who always wore a red rose in his lapel. He questioned me about my new job and asked me if my parents knew about it. I told him they didn't and that I was going to tell them when I got home.

I was so happy I was going to be a ladies' hairdresser; I'd got the job at 'Michele's Ladies

Hairdressers' in Fountain Lane in Belfast – the salon is still there and it's still called Michele's. The two ladies at the salon laughed when I applied for the job; of course I had a lot more hair then, and looking back I might have been the first male ladies' hairdresser in Belfast as it was the early 1960s.

At home, the news wasn't gratefully received, especially by Dickie, but our Ma was always on my side. 'Leave the child alone,' she retorted as she served up the tea, which consisted of champ, ham bones and cabbage.

'Well, I've already handed in my notice to Mr McMahon and I start at Michele's on Monday.'

'Michele's!' Dickie gasped. 'Really wee lad, what do you think you're doing? Your head's cut wanting a job cutting auld dolls' hair.'

I knew then I'd never work as a ladies' hairdresser, but maybe if I had I would have had salons all over the world and several other countries as well, including Fountain Lane in Belfast! Aye, hindsight is a marvellous thing, don't you think?

On Monday morning I went sheepishly back to Stevenson and Turner where my old job as message boy was still waiting for me. I got on my delivery bike and put all thoughts of hairdressing out of my mind. My career in that field was certainly cut short!

Stevenson and Turner was the foremost plumbing and heating company in Belfast and my job was to do wee messages on my black delivery bicycle, with a carrier on the front. It was one of the old-fashioned cycles with a metal stand that pushed forward when the cycle was being ridden.

Travelling one day up Tennant Street, just past the police station, my eyes were drawn to two cracking schoolgirls. I was whistling away at them not watching where I was going. My whistling soon came to an abrupt end; I shortly awoke to discover my bike and I were stuck in the back end of a gleaming baby Austin 7 motor car.

I pulled the bike off the car and discovered, to my horror, two of the neatest, round holes in the back of the car where the stand of the bike had penetrated it. My immediate thoughts were: holy God, this man will kill me. I contemplated this further as I was standing knocking at the door of his house. 'Holy shit, he will kill me; he'll knock my block off.' Away I went, very slowly as if nothing had happened; I can tell you the bike got faster and faster until the tyres became red hot.

I arrived at Belfast Waterworks on the Oldpark Road dripping with sweat. The foreman saw me and said, 'What happened son; did you take a short cut through the dam?' Fortunately, the stopcocks that were in the carrier of my bike were all accounted for, and my whistling days on bikes were soon over.

'George, I want to see you in my office,' I knew by the way Mr McMahon spoke that it wasn't a request. His office was small – a room within a larger office; it had glass partitioned windows so that Mr McMahon could see everything that was going on. We could see him, but only the top of his head and his half-rimmed glasses. I stood in front of him, dressed in my working clothes of jeans and jumper.

'George.'

'Yes, Mr McMahon.'

'What's this about you remonstrating outside the building?' he asked.

'Mr McMahon, I wasn't remonstrating.'

'George, are you telling me lies?' he queried.

'I don't tell lies,' I replied.

'George, you *were* remonstrating, with three boys outside the building, I was told.'

'Do you mean fighting, Mr McMahon?'

'Yes George. Fighting, remonstrating.'

'Oh yes, I was fighting alright! The three bucks spat on my sign.'

He looked at me and asked, 'What sign?'

I told him it was the sign I polished every week; the brass sign at the front door of the building. It was a beautiful brass sign with 'Stevenson and Turner Plumbers Merchants' written into the brass, and every Monday morning I polished it with vigour.

I explained to Mr McMahon that the three cheeky young bucks, about my age, came and spat on my sign, only just after I'd finished polishing it. They were jeering and laughing, but they didn't laugh for long. I beat the crap out of all of them. The boss accepted my apology and I was even promoted to junior salesman in the sanitary department. I think he promoted me to stop any more street fighting.

However, life at Stevenson and Turner was not the same again, especially after the next incident with the salesman Harry Leonard. He accused me of selling a bathroom suite he had promised to the man and lady he was dealing with. I told him I hadn't sold any bathroom suite and he called me a liar, in front of his customers. I gave him a real dig on the chin and said, 'I'm no liar ye old bastard.' I'd knocked him backwards into the latest pink 'Shanks' bath on display in our showroom. He wasn't best pleased, I can tell you! I may be many things, but I'm no liar.

My career as the newly promoted junior sales man in the sanitary department came to an unfortunate end. I really did like working as a salesman for Stevenson and Turner; I could wear a suit, collar and tie, and I felt very posh and important.

Again, I went home jobless and told my Da and Ma I had got the sack. I told them what had happened; my Da asked me why I had hit Mr Leonard, and why I didn't just walk away. I told him it was because he'd called me a liar. I really hadn't sold the bathroom suite; Harry Leonard had sold it himself to another customer and blamed me. He wasn't going to call me a liar, the old shit!

Chapter Two

My Family

'That's it wee lad, you're starting building with us on Monday,' our Sammy said; he was another of my brothers. And so I did, with my brothers Sammy and Alec and my brother-in-law Jackie, who was married to my sister Isobel.

I had five brothers and one sister, all a lot older than me. Our Albert was sixteen years older than me; then came our Jim, Isobel, Dickie, Sammy and Alec – who was seven years my senior. Then there was me. I was born on the thirteenth of July 1946, as a result of my father, Albert Douglas, returning from fighting a vicious war against the Japanese in the Second World War in the jungles of Burma.

My father was serving with the 245 Royal Artillery Eighth Belfast Regiment. He was a slim man of average height, about five feet ten or five feet eleven inches, with dark hair and a dark moustache. He was a very handsome man – well our Ma thought so anyway! He was a strong character, but with a very compassionate side to his nature, and was very fit. He always walked to and from work every day. He worked as a house repairer and was later promoted to a caretaker for a Technical College in North Howard Street Mill. I loved our Da.

Before the war, and even after the war, it was very difficult to make ends meet. Ma didn't go out to work; she had enough to do taking care of all of us. Home was a wee kitchen house, two up and two down, at number fourteen Wigton Street in Belfast, which was situated between the Shankill Road and the Falls Road, the two most notorious areas in Belfast and have seen some of the most vicious and sectarian murders in the world.

In order to make ends meet, my father and his older brother, Jim Douglas, who was also known as 'gentleman Jim', used to bare-fist fight for extra money. This was during the 'hungry thirties' when people were on the Government outdoor relief allowance. Da and Uncle Jim were well known in a place called the Chapel Fields in Belfast, where the bare-fist fighting took place. The fights mostly took place on Sundays when men would gather together, hold each other's coat and take their turn in the bare-fist fights. These were hard men living in hard times.

The fights were illegal, of course, and were organised by a woman known as Ma Copley; she owned an ice-cream shop in Divis Street in Belfast, which is a continuation of the Falls Road. Da and Uncle Jim were lightweight fighters, but they would have fought anyone of any weight for money, and that's what they did to raise money to feed their families.

I remember on one occasion my Da telling me that he and my Uncle Jim had walked from the Shankill Road to a small town fourteen miles away, called Ballyclare. They arrived at a farm and in a small cowshed a number of men had come down from the surrounding countryside to bare-fist fight. They used to fight ten rounds at a time, for money, and again they would have fought any man at any weight for the extra money. They normally got about one week's pay, which was about £4 to £5. Uncle Jim sustained quite a few injuries in these horrendous fights; he had two cauliflower ears and a broken nose. Da had a broken nose on a number of occasions, and cut eyes and lips.

Although my father fought and was strong he would never lift his hands to me or to any of my brothers. No matter what trouble I was in, my Da only had to give me one of his 'looks' and that was that. It was my Ma who gave us the hidings if we got out of line.

My mother was a robust, small woman with plenty of 'spirit'. She was about five feet three inches tall, dark brown hair and blue eyes. She had a heart as big as the world and always had time for people; she was the first to offer help when people were in trouble.

There was an auld critter called Geordie Burrows (all George's were nicknamed 'Geordie' in those days in Northern Ireland). Geordie used to walk down the middle of the street singing rebel songs and people used to give him a few pence; he was cute though – if he walked down the street in Republican areas he would sing Republican songs and in Protestant areas he sang Protestant songs. He was a fat wee man with bale twine wrapped around his dirty old coat and wore an old 'paddy' hat.

My mother didn't have money to give him, but she gave him other things that were more beneficial to him than money. She would ask him to sit on the windowsill outside the house and gave him a bowl of soup, and sometimes she would give him a bowl of stew and a huge lump of bread. I remember he used to say 'God Bless you Bella'. Her full name was Isabella Kane Douglas, but my Da called her Bella. She was a very kind and understanding woman and very tough; if my Ma said you hadn't to do something, you just didn't dare do it.

My mother's parents, my Granda and Granny Kane, whose names were Sam and Sarah, were both down-to-earth working-class people. My Granny Kane was a real businesswoman. She owned her own fruit and vegetable shop in a wee side street off the Shankill Road. The area was known in those days as 'The Banjo'.

I remember my Granny as a tall big chested woman with grey hair, who you would never give 'back cheek' to; she would have hit you a clout on the ear if you got in her way. I suppose you could say that she ran the first ever 'carry out' business in Belfast. She would make pots of jacket potatoes, pots of cabbage with ham bones and shanks that she got from 'Lipton's' grocers shop on the Shankill Road. People who hadn't time to make their own dinner would order their food from my Granny; the only stipulation Granny made was that the pots all had to be returned spotless.

Granda Kane was a small man about five feet four inches. He looked like the film star Victor McLaughlin who starred in 'The Quiet Man' with John Wayne and Maureen O'Hara. Granda was a quiet man – he had to be living with Granny Kane. He was a 'well diviner' and travelled throughout Ireland sinking wells for folk. In those days, sinking wells was done by hand – there were no JCB diggers to help out. You had to be tough with arms and hands like shovels.

When Granda returned from digging wells at the weekends, he liked nothing better than putting his feet up in front of the turf and coal fire and smoking his pipe. However, his peace was short lived whenever Granny started making her boiled sweets and 'yellow man', which was like a form of honeycomb. She used to get Granda to cut up the long lengths of toffee into bite-size pieces and put each one into a penny sweet bag. These were called 'lucky bags' because Granny put a 'wing', which was one penny, into one in every twenty bags. I had another name for them; I called them 'Wee Geordie's lucky bags' because, out of the three pence pocket money my Granda gave me, my Granny made me spend one penny in her shop. I made sure I knew which bag contained the 'wing'. My pocket money was then reduced 'cos Granny caught me 'hoaking' through the lucky bags; I got a good whacking and that was the end of that.

I didn't know my Granda and Granny Douglas, but I do know my Grandfather Douglas was born in Scotland, but left there when he was a young man. He went to live in England where he met my Grandmother whose name was Brown. Both my paternal grandparents were deaf and could not speak. My Da and Uncle Jim were both born in England, but moved to Northern Ireland when they were young boys. Stories are told that Granda Douglas could never keep a job down and he felt that people were laughing at him. He used to get frustrated with this and would often end up fighting. I suppose it was difficult for him.

As the war in Europe escalated, my parents became increasingly worried about the wellbeing of the children. My father had the presence of mind to rent a small house in the country. The idea was that while he was away fighting the war, Ma would take my brothers and sister to the country house in the event of Germans bombing Belfast.

Belfast had one of the biggest shipbuilding yards in the world, Harland and Wolff, and also a large aircraft factory, Short Brothers and Harland. This borne in mind, on Easter Monday of 1940 the German Luftwaffe bombed Belfast. The bombs rained down on our city causing devastation and much heartache and bloodshed.

Typical of our Ma, she had taken all my brothers and sister to Belfast Zoo for the holiday; that was something people did in Belfast. Easter time was always a busy time at the zoo. Ma told me how they all ran for it when they heard the bombs and saw the planes flying overhead. My family lived in the West Belfast area, and the zoo was in North Belfast, about four miles away. They had to catch a bus to the town centre. Most people were running away from the town centre, but not our family. They had an uncanny knack of running into danger when others were running away from it.

My family then lived at number sixty-nine Joseph Street, just below my Granny Kane's shop. Fortunately, they all arrived at Granny Kane's safe and well. Everyone scurried under the shop counter, which was made of marble, and my Granny piled mattresses on the top and over the front of it. They were all petrified and started praying to God for help.

The very next day, with their prayers answered and with all their belongings, they managed to get a lift in a truck and off they went to the country house at Mildbush, Carrick Fergus. Night after night they sat in the hedgerows on the hill behind the house watching the Germans bombing the shit out of Belfast.

It is my understanding that there were more bombs dropped on our city than there were dropped in Coventry. A few months later, Ma and the children became evacuees to a place called Stewart Hall at Stewartstown in County Tyrone; there they remained until the end of the war.

Our father was still in Burma. His regiment's task was to engage the Japanese as they tried to cross Burma to India. He wrote as often as he could to our mother to let us know developments. The letters were read to Ma by my eldest brother, Albert, as Ma couldn't read or write. She was good at figures though because she had been working in my Granny's shop. Albert then had to reply to Da's letters at my mother's dictation. For the many families whose husbands, fathers and sons had volunteered to fight for their country, the times were hard for all who were left behind, with uncertainty of them not returning.

Chapter Three

The Early Years

The war years had ended and I was born in 1946. My family had already moved into Wigton Street from Joseph Street. The house was a small kitchen house in the middle of a long terraced row of about thirty houses on each side of the narrow street. The road outside was cobbled and the footpaths were tiled in a raised diamond pattern. Ma always kept her doorstep clean; you could see the half-moon shape around the step where she continually washed it down.

The only car in the street belonged to my uncle, Billy Fittis, who lived across the road from us. He was married to my mother's sister, my Aunt Violet. In those days you were very posh if you had a car, and I remember I was very proud 'cos he was my uncle and I would tell all my friends that he had a car. It was an Austin car, two-tone grey and maroon with leather upholstery.

My first recollection of riding in that car was when I was about three or four years old. It was a lovely sunny day and Uncle Billy took me, my Da, my Uncle Geordie

(Ma's brother) and John Thompson, my cousin, to a place called Millisle in County Down. We all went down to the beach and collected a whole bucket full of 'wellicks' (winkles). We would pick the wellicks from the rocks and seaweed that remained on the shore when the tide had gone out. I remember that day well, even though I was very young; it somehow stuck in my memory.

We arrived home at teatime. The wellicks were washed and scrubbed clean and placed in the bucket that we put on the stove where they boiled until tender. You didn't boil them too much 'cos they would have got too hard.

The following day everyone was out of the house. I was on my own and Ma was across the street with my Aunt Violet. I saw the wellicks sitting there on the sink. The water had been poured away. I got a pin from Ma's workbox and started to devour each wellick one by one. I put the pin end into the eye of the wellick and 'hoaked' it out savouring the flavour of the seaside where we were the day before. I ate half the bucket of wellicks while I was home alone and, my word, did I pay for my greed!

I was admitted to Purdysburn Fever Hospital on the Saintfield Road in Belfast. I had taken dysentery and, boy, was I ill! I was placed in the isolation room that was surrounded with glass windows. When my Da and Ma came to visit me they could only look at me through the glass partition. I couldn't have any contact with anyone. I remember my bed was a high-sided cot. I could just rest my chin on the sides as I looked out to the glass partition where my parents were. I used to cry a lot and felt like I was totally abandoned. Oh how I longed to get to the other side of the glass and have a hug from my Ma! I was in the hospital for between three and four weeks, but it seemed an eternity

Ma came to collect me when I was discharged. She had brought me a grand black gabardine coat with a belt to wear going home from the hospital. I felt so special; I'd never had a gabardine coat before. I also had a new pair of sandals. Ma hadn't bought the coat but had borrowed it from Matt Thompson who was a distant cousin of our family. He lived three doors below us in Wigton Street. I didn't want to give the coat back and caused so much fuss that my Da promised he'd buy me one of my own.

The wellick incident was my first recollection of life, and also my first recollection of near death. I haven't touched wellicks since!

The feeling of being left alone when I was in hospital remained with me throughout part of my early years, although my family were all loving and caring towards me. I never saw or heard my brothers or our Isobel arguing or fighting; each one cared about the other and we were happiest when each other was doing well. I was, you could say, a bit of a tearaway. I was spoilt by all of them, being the youngest. In fact, I used to play one off against the other, especially if they gave me money. If our Albert gave me sixpence, I'd tell our Sammy I'd got a shilling; he would then give me a shilling. It was just dead easy – what a horror I was!

When I was a youngster Granda Kane would take me everywhere with him. He liked to get away from my Granny to get a bit of peace and quiet. I always got treats from him, like going to the ice-cream shop and going general shopping together.

One special time with Granda was visiting the Alambra picture house in Lower North Street in Belfast. The picture house was a beautiful building; I think it used to be a real theatre. It was built in the Victorian era with elaborate balconies and cornices on the ceiling. It had three floors and the middle floor was a licensed bar.

We'd gone to see my first ever film. Charlie Chaplin was in it and I felt a very big man going with my Granda. I was only four and we stayed in the bar watching the whole film. I sat on the end of the bar dressed in my short trousers, hob-nailed boots, white shirt and braces and my wee tweed coat and cap. Granda bought me a 'Cola' drink and I drank out of the neck of the bottle. I suppose you could say I was the first ever 'Yuppie' as this was 1950!

Granda always wore a cap and a white muffler scarf. I can see him now in his tweed suit drinking his pint of Porter (*Guinness*) as I drank my Cola, just like Victor McLaughlin in 'The Quiet Man'. Although my Granda took me to the cinema, I don't remember who took who home, between me being high on Cola and Granda high on Guinness.

On our return, Granny Kane bellowed at him, 'Where the hell have you been with that child?' Granda

27

told her where we'd been but, as usual, Granny shouted at him anyway.

I attended Riddle Memorial primary school at the age of five years. My class teacher was a lady by the name of Miss Stick. There were two teachers, wee Miss Stick and big Miss Stick, they were sisters. Wee Miss Stick taught the younger children and big Miss Stick the older children; she was older as well. I was sat beside a wee fella called Billy. We sat at a long desk together on an equally long form; they were both joined together. The desk and the form were made of wood and both had carvings scratched into them by the many children before us.

Billy McCormack was a nice boy, although a bit on the slow side. The bugger kept pissing himself, wetting his pants through. But that wasn't all; he pissed on the form and his pee used to run along and wet my backside through. His pants would then dry while he was still wearing them. Boy, did he smell!

In the early 1950s each child in primary school was allocated a gill of milk (one third of a pint) at break time. It seemed to me whenever Billy had his milk drunk, he always wet himself. Eventually I made the decision to tell Miss Stick and I put my hand in the air to get her attention. She was very angry with Billy and sent him out of the classroom. I could see she had made him feel bad. I didn't like Billy feeling like that, as he couldn't help what he had been doing.

This went on for quite a while. Every day Billy would wet himself. Every day I'd get my backside wet.

But I'd devised a plan - I now had it cracked. When I asked to go to the toilet I took Billy with me, and that saved us both getting wet. Miss Stick also caught on to my logic and so Billy and I always went to the toilet together after our milk break; guess what? No more wetting.

I quite enjoyed school; I liked history and geography and seemed to do well at these subjects, but I was always ready to have a bit of fun.

On one occasion I took my pet mouse to school. He was snowy white and I called him 'Herbie'. Miss Stick saw me lifting the lid of my desk; Herbie was in there having his breakfast of digestive biscuits. I was feeding him wee crumbs.

'Geordie Douglas, what are you doing with the lid of your desk up?'

'Nothing, Miss Stick,' I replied.

'You're at something, so bring me whatever it is up here.'

'It's nothing Miss,' I said.

'Just bring it up here when you're told,' she shouted sternly.

I put Herbie in my right-hand trouser pocket. I kept him in my hand because my pocket had a hole in it.

'What have you got in your pocket Geordie?' Miss Stick asked quietly when I reached the front of the class.

'Show me what you have in there, now.'

I took Herbie out of my pocket and opened my hand carefully. Well, all hell broke loose as wee Herbie escaped and ran all around the classroom floor. Miss Stick freaked out; I don't actually think she was too keen on white mice!

She jumped onto her desk; as did some of the young girls in the class, but poor Herbie met an unfortunate death when he came into contact with the hobnail boot of a wee buck in our class who kicked him so hard he flew up and hit the blackboard. Poor Herbie! We had been friends for a long time and he always came to school with me. However, I did give him a full 'mouse funeral'; rest in peace Herbie!

It was a sad day, particularly so because of Herbie. I left school with a heavy heart anyway, besides having to put up with getting a good 'slapping' from John Bailey on the way home.

He was such a bully, he was the school bully! It seemed like every day on my way home John Bailey was there at the corner of Malvern Street. He used to come over to me and pull my school coat down over my arms so it restricted my movements. Then he continued to slap me about the face and head…for no reason at all.

He was two years older than me and was a fat boy, he obviously didn't like me but I had never done anything to him.

On this day I finally broke down and when he let me go I ran like hell to my house. I couldn't wait to get in to see Ma she would make everything 'alright'. I was greeted by my black Labrador, 'Laddie' who always waited at the top of our street for me when I came home from school. I loved Laddie and he loved me and seemed distressed because he knew I was upset as we ran home together.

Ma was always at the house when I arrived home from school. It was unknown for her not to greet me with kind words and to have some of her delicious homemade soda bread or rock buns ready for me. I valued those times. There would be just the two of us at home, prior to my brothers and sister Isabel coming home from school and work.

I was given a long rein by my parents and was spoilt by my siblings. I suppose it was because there was such an age gap between our Alec and me. Arriving home from school, as usual, I entered the house. I always shouted 'Hey Ma,' and my Ma always shouted back, 'Yes wee son'; that's all I needed; just to hear her voice and I was re-assured she was home.

'Hey Ma?' I shouted; there was silence. I went from room to room frantically shouting for her. Where was she, what had happened? I started to get frightened and angry, and without a thought for anyone but myself, I started to wreck the house. I knocked all the plants off the side-board, threw my schoolbag into the corner of the room, knocked the 'mother-in-law's tongue' plant over, spilling the soil onto Ma's nice clean floor, and gave 'Twinkle', our cat, a kick up the arse. All the while shouting 'Where the fuck are you Ma?'

Suddenly she was behind me. Without a word of warning she gave me a slap across my ear; she nearly knocked my head off. 'How dare you kick that cat? Don't you dare to do that again.' She sent me to bed with the threat not to show my face downstairs again that day, nor was I getting any tea. I never got my tea or any of her homemade soda that day, nor did our Laddie.

I missed not being able to join the rest of the family at teatime that day. Everyone wanted to know where I was, and of course Ma told them of my escapade. I loved sitting at the table 'ear-wigging' their conversations of what they had all done at work and school during the day.

Ma must have told our Da how naughty I had been that night because later he came to my room and I was still crying.

'What's up son?' Da said, he had a quiet way with him and that made me cry even more. I eventually told him about what had happened to 'Herbie' and my unfortunate meetings with John Bailey on the way home from school. I blurted it all out to him.

'This is what you do Geordie,' Da said as he gave me a small thick cosh-like baton. It was quite heavy and dense. 'You put this up your sleeve and when John Bailey does this to you again you work the cosh down your sleeve and give him a whack with it. He won't do it again to you wee lad.'

Da then asked, 'Why are you letting him do this too you Geordie?' I told him it was because I was frightened of him and he had a broken nose. Da said, 'Well he can't be that good if he's got a broken nose.'

I can't remember if it was the next day or not but I got my chance and Bailey definitely got his comeuppance.

'Slap, slap, slap', I endured one or two slaps. Now it was my turn. I slid the cosh down my right sleeve of my jumper underneath my coat. My arms were still restricted but I had enough movement to whack him over the head. That made him stop slapping me as he didn't know where the whack had come from. He looked around him and as he did so I gave him another two whacks with the cosh and he immediately let me go. He ran away bleeding and holding his head. He wondered what had hit him. I was elated. Da was right, he never did it too me again and when I saw him on my way home from school he always crossed over to the other side of the road.

I was reported to the police and the school but I didn't care. He got what he deserved and I became the hero of the school and was asked to stop fights in the playground.

There was only me, Alex and our Sammy at school, the rest were all working. Albert, my oldest brother, was a joiner and was excellent at what he did. Jim was a painter and did a lot of graining; that is painting surfaces to make them look like natural wood. Dickie was a fitter with an engineering company, prior to him joining the Merchant Navy, and our Isobel worked in the mill. They were all very conscientious about their jobs and worked very hard.

Sammy was the academic member of the family. He was the only child in his year to pass the qualifying examination to go to Grammar School. Sadly, he couldn't go; my parents couldn't afford the PE kit, let alone the uniform.

Meal times were when we all got together around the table to have some of Ma's special dinners; sometimes it was delicious liver and bacon with mashed potatoes, or herrings with new potatoes and buttermilk to drink. There were a lot of hungry mouths to feed. Ma would get through at least one stone of potatoes a day with all us lot. Potatoes were boiled, champed (with spring onions or scallions as we called them), fried, chipped and baked, and there was always dessert of apple pie, rhubarb and apple, bread and butter pudding, dumpling and custard or sherry trifle. We always had plenty of good food in our bellies. Ma was a great baker; Granny Kane taught her when they had the shop.

When dinner arrived I always got mine first and the others were told by Ma to, 'Let the child get his first.'

My brothers would shout back, 'Hurry up wee lad and stop mucking about.' It's no wonder I thought I was more important than anyone else. My place at the table was at the right-hand side of my Ma, but to be honest I felt I should have been sitting at the top of the table, the most important place, or so I thought.

Topics of conversation around our tea table varied enormously. Albert and Jim were cyclists and used to do a lot of road racing. In fact, Albert held the Northern Ireland record for a 25-mile road race in one hour and one minute. It wasn't broken for quite a number of years. One topic of conversation was always creeping up, the war and how Ma and everyone else who were visiting the zoo one day had to run for their lives out of the zoo.

I was fed up not contributing to the conversation and said, 'I can laugh at all of yous; while you were hiding under granny's shop counter, where was I?' There was silence and they all looked at me with amazement. 'Well, where was I?' I repeated to them.

Our Dickie replied, 'You weren't even here wee lad.'

'Exactly,' I said, 'that's because I was with our Da, fighting the Japanese hand to hand in the Burmese jungle, when you were hiding under my granny's counter.' There was huge laughter. After they all settled down I carried on to say, 'I don't want to hear any more of your stories about hiding under granny's counter.' I certainly knew where I had come from and still believe I was fighting the war to this day.

Meal times were a real squash around our crowded table, so much so we occasionally had to have meals in two sittings. They were happy times. I look back with fondness at Isobel and my brothers and how kind they were to me. Our kitchen house was only very small; downstairs there was a small kitchen scullery and a living room where we all ate our meals. Ma and Da's bedroom was also just off the living room, and just big enough for a wardrobe, side table and a double bed. The fire in the living room heated the whole house; there was no central heating then. My, there were some cold winter days, but when we were all gathered around the fire we had some chat. There were two bedrooms upstairs. I shared a double bed with our Isobel and my brothers all shared the other upstairs bedroom. Albert slept in the top bunk and Jim underneath, Dickie, Alec and Sammy all shared a double bed.

Our Isobel always made me go to bed first to warm up the bed. When she came up, more often than not she had a box of chocolates, Black Magic or Cadbury's Dairy Milk, which she used to share with me. Her boyfriend, Jackie, bought them for her. She would stuff my mouth with the ones she didn't like, such as the ginger chocolates and the orange and strawberry creams; I would rather have had the caramels or nutty ones, but no such luck, she ate all those.

Our bedroom was also sparse, just shiny oilcloth on the floor. It had a fireplace and if anyone took sick Ma

35

would sometimes light a fire in there. On the floors downstairs there were rush mats laid over the top of the oilcloth. Isobel always gave the house a good clean every Monday night and she would place newspaper under the rush mats to catch any dust and dirt.

Dickie was a young entrepreneur. He was eighteen years old and he had his own allotment on the Cave Hill Road. He grew vegetables and flowers; he sold the flowers door-to-door for 'a bob a bunch'. People complained that the flowers had no fragrance so he used to spray the heads with Isobel's scent. His daffodils would smell of lavender and his chrysanthemums of lily of the valley! I remember Dickie coming home from work one day and saying, 'Hey Ma, I bought our wee Geordie a suit from Spackmans.' Everybody and their granny went to Spackmans to get a suit. 'I've put a deposit down.' I told everyone our Dickie had bought me my first ever suit; I was over the moon. I got the suit that week and I was the only wee lad in the street to have one. But the suit wasn't very long lived; two weeks later I ripped the arse out of it.

My brothers Alex and Sammy were in the Scouts. They would go camping up into the big glen not far from our home. I was too young to join the scouts, so I couldn't go with them. But, oh how I longed to join in with all the fun they used to have. On Sundays, Alec and Sammy would walk up the glen to a place we all knew called 'hookie fa nookie'; it was just a part of the glen where the local kids met with each other. It was a beautiful area with a small waterfall. My brothers had tied a long rope to an old oak tree close to the river and they took turns sitting on the large knot at the end of the rope and then swinging out across the river. Sometimes they would light fires, like they did with the Scouts, and make tea in a National Dried Milk container over the fire. When the fire turned to hot grey and red ashes, they baked potatoes in their jackets and cooked sausages, which they had pinched from Ma's larder, and the meal was thoroughly enjoyed when eaten round the camp fire.

I suppose I was a bit of a nuisance to our Alex and Sammy because I was quite a bit younger than them. I always wanted to go up the glen with them but they said I was too much trouble and so they adopted devious means to avoid me. They used to sneak out of the house when they thought I wasn't watching them, but I knew when they were going out.

'Are you going up the glen today?' I would ask.

'No wee lad, we're staying in today,' they lied. 'We're getting our Scouts stuff ready for Monday night.'

I knew they would be going then, especially when the both of them huddled outside in the toilet talking for absolutely ages, planning for their getaway. The next indication I would get was, 'Geordie, go and get us two penny bars of chocolate from the shop.' With the money in my hand I was away to get the chocolate as fast as I could. I knew they had left the house quickly to try to get away from me. Of course I knew which way they were heading; they went the same way and I always followed them, but I also knew a short cut.

Keeping them in sight, I followed them a long way. Only when we reached the glen did I let them know I'd followed on behind them, taking care not to be spotted. They wouldn't send me home now as it was too far for me to go alone. Our Ma would have been very upset with them and I knew it.

'What are you doing wee lad?' Alex gasped, and with that grabbed me by the throat and shook me like a rag doll. 'You're a bloody nuisance, so you are. When are you going to do what you're told? I'm gonna tell my Ma on you.'

'Don't you want your chocolate bars then?' I spluttered.

'Give us them,' they both shouted at me.

I gave them only the one chocolate bar and told them the other bar had melted; they didn't believe me and I then got another shaking.

'We're away,' they mocked. 'You'll not be able to keep up with us and the auld lad will get you.' The auld lad was some mythical being from the glen but, no worries, the auld lad, whoever he was, wasn't as tough as me! However, I started to cry in order to get some sympathy, but it didn't work. Off they marched like lightning with me racing along behind them in order to keep up, which I did.

Once at the glen, I was able to join in the fun. In fact, they had no choice, they knew they couldn't shake me off. I was only about six but had plenty of wit.

'One day you're gonna get yourself lost and hurt wee lad; you won't listen to what you're told and you have to be tough to do what we do.'

'I am tough,' I replied.

'No you're not, you're only a wee lad, but come on, keep up,' our Sammy laughed. They then made me do everything they did. I learnt to make fires, tie different scout knots and make shelters.

'You have to jump the river Geordie, same as us,' Alec challenged. 'Then you can come with us all the time.' They knew, and I knew, that the river at the green gate, where we were, was too wide for me to jump. Alec jumped across easily as he was more agile than Sammy, who was more robust and had shorter legs.

'It's too wide and deep for me,' I said.

'You have to jump Geordie, or you won't come with us again,' Alec shouted from the opposite bank. Still wearing my new Sunday suit our Dickie had bought me the week before, I walked up the river bank until I saw a narrower place to cross. I ran up to the river and jumped across, sinking into the soft mud at the far side. My socks and sandals left my feet and stuck in the mud and my feet were stinking, but oh, deep joy. I'd made it now. I felt as good as them. I ran towards them carrying my socks and sandals and they had the cheek to say I was cheating. I pointed out to them they did not specify exactly where I had to cross the river, only that I must cross.

'You're a wee cheat,' Sammy exclaimed. He still hadn't jumped across but was about to do so.

With the large pack on his back he leaped over the river, landing on the grassy bank on the other side. But fate was not on his side; the heavy pack he was carrying dragged him backwards and in he fell. Well, I was in stitches. I just roared laughing at him and shouted 'ha, ha, you can't come with us now, only me and our Alec can go!' With his face like thunder and steam blaring from his nostrils he emerged from the river like a roaring bull, charging towards me. I was away like a whippet across the fields. I gave him a wide berth all day and stayed out of his way.

We all made our way home across the face of Divis Mountain, passing a landmark farm that everybody knew as 'Uncle Bob's Farm'. He used to milk his goats in his kitchen – lovely!

Sammy and Alec went ahead of me and made their way back through the glen and down a very steep bank, with me following behind as usual. The bank was very steep, so much so that I slipped and tumbled down the gravel bank and ripped the arse out of my new suit. I cut my legs, arms and elbows and I was totally covered in muck. The suit was ruined and I looked as if I'd just come back from the trenches.

My brothers started panicking and sucking up to me, pleading for me not to tell Ma that I had been with them because I was hurt and my suit was ruined. They knew they were in for a whacking, as our Ma would have blamed them for not looking after me. They promised me all sorts of inducements, sweets and ice cream, if I didn't tell our Ma. Now I was one of them and I could go to the glen with them any time I wanted to.

When I got home I expected the good hiding that Ma gave me for ruining my new suit. Alec and Sammy witnessed the hiding and I could see their eyes getting bigger and bigger, dreading me telling Ma I was with them. But not me, I was thinking too much of the lovely inducements of sweets and ice cream to ever tell my Ma. As she whacked out at me, I ducked and dived the blows; she only connected with me a couple of times. 'That's the last suit you're getting wee lad; you're a disgrace.' I'd had a few whackings from my Ma so I'd learnt how to duck and dive each blow.

After the dust had settled I quietly reminded Alex and Sammy of the promises they had made. Alec reminded me I'd already had one bar of chocolate and to stop nattering on at them. I kept on, as only I would have done, and told them that if they didn't pony up, I would tell Ma about the day up the glen. They soon 'ponied' up and I gorged myself on a slider of ice cream stuffed with a Cadburys milk flake down the middle. As I licked my lips, the memories of the hiding Ma gave me faded away.

I was now in the big boys' league. I'd learnt a lot from Sammy and Alec, albeit with a lot of reluctance on their part.

It was when I asked them, and they promised, to teach me to swim I got my just desserts. We all three went to the Falls swimming baths for my first swimming lesson, and little did I know my first lesson in survival. Once at the poolside, Alec and Sammy took hold of an arm each and hurled me head first into the six feet deep end of the pool, narrowly missing the diving board as I entered the depth beyond. My arms and legs thrashed about in the deep water as I was desperately trying to reach the sanctity of the poolside that got nearer and nearer until I grabbed the stone lip at the edge. I could just about breathe again, and as I rubbed my eyes I could see my brothers laughing uncontrollably at me. 'I thought you promised to teach me to swim, not nearly drown me,' I choked at them.

'Didn't we just do that? You swam over to the side, didn't you?' our Sammy laughed. They got their bitter sweet revenge that day and they also convinced me I could swim. I feared nothing now – I knew everything, or so I thought!

I knew I was a bit of a nuisance to Alec and Sammy but one Saturday morning they must have eaten their words.

It was a lovely bright day and I was in the street playing 'marlies' (marbles) with my mates. I saw my Ma's sister Aunt Susie walk into the front door of our house. She didn't get the whole way in and came back out shouting, 'Fire fire!' She was hysterical. I bolted up the street and entered the house by the front door, underneath the smoke which by now was rising up towards the bedrooms. No-one was in the downstairs of the house as our Ma had gone to the shops. I couldn't get upstairs because of the smoke. I was only 8 years old but I was switched on. I ran like lightning to the top of our street and to the corner of Northumberland Street and the Shankill Road, where the fire alarm was.

In those days each area had a red cast iron fire alarm standing on its own in the footpath. I picked up a stone on the waste ground and smashed the glass of the alarm and pulled the handle out towards. It must have worked as within five minutes two big red Belfast fire engines came roaring down the Shankill Road from Ardoyne. The driver shouted at me, 'Did you pull that handle wee lad?'

I shouted back, 'Yes Mister our fucking house is on fire.' He told me to jump onto the fire engine and hold tight with both hands (no health and safety there). 'Turn right here Mister, in Northumberland Street,' I said as I directed the firemen down to my house at Wigton Street.

A piece of coal had fallen from the fire onto the hearth and my dad's slippers caught fire. In turn they set fire to the valence on the chair and then the chair itself caught fire causing the cupboard beside it to burn.

All this time unbeknown to me our Alec and Sammy were upstairs in bed having a Saturday morning 'lie in'. When the fire was out they came walking downstairs with their faces as black as night. They told me they survived by putting their heads out of the upstairs window. In my own mind I believe I saved their lives by calling the fire brigade when I did ... they owed me once again!

I had conquered the glen and I could swim and now I had saved my brothers lives! Now, nothing could now stand in my way. My gang and I would go up to the glen. I was their leader; so carrying an empty milk tin, loose tea and sugar mixed together, potatoes and sausages, we went off on our own adventure without older brothers to aggravate me.

We were all wee lads who lived in the same streets close to one another and we would visit the glen on several occasions in the good weather. This particular day though, put an end finally to my adventurous days up the glen. The encounter I hadn't planned for and nor had some of the other wee lads.

Part of the fun for us all was selecting large stones from the surrounding grassy mounds on the Black Mountain and sending them rolling down the steep hill on the lower slopes. The object was to see whose stone reached the bottom first. Situated at the bottom of the hill was a row of very pretty white washed cottages with their back gardens facing the steep hill. Unbeknown to us, our large stones were hurtling down the hill and hitting the back wall of the cottages.

A young man who was probably in his early twenties, with fair hair and wearing blue denim dungarees, came out of one of the cottages and shouted at us to come down the hill. The five of us came slowly down to join him. He was very angry and he gave us two choices. Neither of them appealed to us. 'Right you wee bucks,' he spat out at us, 'the first choice you have is that I phone the police and get you all arrested, and they will probably fine you five pounds, or I beat you all with a stick and that will be the end of it.'

I thought about it and said, 'Mister, you better beat me, and those two wee bucks as well, 'cos their Ma has no money either.' I was referring to Billie Leslie, who we used to call 'porky', and his younger brother Tommy.

The man took us away from the cottages to a place near some bushes where we had never been before. We had to stand in a line, and when it was our turn to be beaten we had to drop our trousers. The man then fastened our hands together with our braces and tied us to a stump of a fallen tree. He gave us five whacks each with the branch of a tree, except for me – I got eight whacks 'cos I was the oldest boy. We were all crying and yelping from the pain. I was the last to be whacked, and was I sore? 'Now don't be coming back here or you'll get the same again,' the man promised us. He let us go then and we ran like hell to our homes, promising each other not to tell our parents. The man had really hurt us and left large welts on our backs and bums. Alas, the poor Johnson brothers were getting bathed for church the following day and their Ma saw the welts on their wee bodies and they had to tell their Ma what had happened.

I hadn't told my Ma or Da about the whackings we had got. It was only when Mrs Johnson came round to our house that the full story unfolded. 'Has your Geordie been given a beating?' Mrs Johnson asked Ma.

'Did someone give you a beating wee son?' Ma asked me. I just looked at her and she asked me again, 'Geordie, did someone give you a beating?'

'I'm all right Ma,' I assured her. 'We'd all have been fined five pounds if we hadn't got the beating and we don't have that sort of money.' I told her why we had been beaten and how the man gave us the two options, a beating or telling the police. Then she took me into the scullery while Mrs Johnson waited in the living room. Ma saw the welts on my back and was shocked. She started to cry and I was so sorry making Ma cry. I felt desperate about that. I explained who the man was and said that he lived in one of the white cottages.

When my Da saw the welts on my body the following day he took Uncle Jim and Uncle Dan, his brothers, to try and find the man, but they didn't find him. It was just as well as they would have killed him. On the Monday morning my mates and I were taken down to Hastings Street police station, near Divis Street, to report the matter. I laugh now; it must have been a comical sight to see five wee bucks with their trousers down and all stood in a line showing the policeman our backsides. The first 'full monty' ever! The policeman, I could see, was really angry, not at us but at the person who did this to us. He was never caught and I didn't dare go back there. I suppose I learnt my lesson for now anyway and my days of adventure up that glen were well and truly over.

Wee Geordie's Parents

Isabella, Albert, sister Isobel, brothers Alex and Sammy with Wee Geordie the cowboy.

Chapter Four

The Special School

At the age of seven years, Ma noticed a change in me. I was eating less food and slowly losing weight. I was coughing and was so run down that she took me to the doctor, who in turn sent me along to a specialist.

Tuberculosis, known in those days as consumption, was rampant throughout the Belfast area. It was believed I had contracted the disease although this was not confirmed. Tuberculosis was a contagious disease of the lungs and was passed on easily when people were coughing and spluttering.

As a precaution, the specialist recommended that I attend Graymount, an open-air school on the Shore Road in Belfast. The open-air school was a place where children were sent who had ill-health, where emphasis was placed on recovery as opposed to the academic side of schooling. When I heard the doctor say this I started to cry. Ma asked me why I was crying. 'Why is that man sending me to a home Ma, when I haven't done anything wrong?' I asked her sobbing.

'It's not a home wee son, it's like a hospital and it will make you better,' she replied.

I still wasn't convinced that it wasn't a home for bad boys, and all the way home I was rhyming on at Ma saying, 'You ole fucker, you're sending me off to a home when I haven't done anything wrong.'

'I've told you before, I'm not sending you to a home; it's like a hospital – but listen Geordie, if you don't stop cursing I will send you to a home.' She then tried to explain to me that our Dickie had been to Graymount when he was younger because they thought he had tuberculosis.

I couldn't wait until our Dickie came home from work that day. I was running in and out of the house making a real nuisance of myself; *I was just dying to find out about the school.* When Dickie arrived home I bombarded him with questions. 'Hey Dickie, did our Ma send you to a home?' I spat out to him.

'No, she did not; what makes you say that wee lad?' our Dickie replied with a puzzled expression.

'Because the fucker is sending me to one,' I said.

Ma heard our conversation and she came out of the kitchen and said, 'I've told you before and I'm tired of telling you, it's not a home, it's a health school you're going to.'

'I'm going to tell our Da you're sending me to a home,' I rattled on.

'Dickie, will you tell him it's not a home, but I will send him to one if he doesn't stop that bad talk.'

Our Dickie sat me down and explained that the open-air school would make me better and I would have my own gardening plot where I could grow my own vegetables. He told me all the children were given a cup of cocoa in the mornings when they arrived at school and the dinners were very good too. I would also get my own bed and blanket, because in the afternoon we would go to bed for a wee rest. 'Why do they make you go to bed when you're not tired?' I asked. Dickie explained that the children went to bed for a rest after lunch in order to help them get well again. He continued to tell me also that I mustn't use bad talk, even though the other wee bucks in the street used it. The 'F' word was commonly used in everyday life in the streets where I grew up.

Dickie convinced me that the special school was a special place and I would learn far more there than any other school. He told me it was like having a school out in the countryside. 'You like going out into the country and going up the glen don't you?' he asked. I told him I did. 'Well then, this school is like being in the middle of the country, you'll love it.' Now I just couldn't wait to start; I knew that I was special and now I was going to a school that was special.

The week prior to starting at Graymount I was off school. Ma had bought me a brand new matching tweed coat and cap. She had to borrow the money from Mr Waterman, the Jew; he was a moneylender. You borrowed the money from him and paid him back each week. It was called 'tick'. I couldn't wait for Monday morning to come so I could get to wearing my new coat and cap.

The Wednesday before I started Graymount was a wet day. I was in the living room poking the fire when a knock came to the door. 'Ma,' I shouted, 'there's someone at the door.'

Ma was in the scullery baking. 'Go and see who it is then,' she replied, her hands full of flour. I opened our front door and was confronted by a tall man wearing a 'paddy' hat and he had a big camera round his neck. He was knocking at all the doors along the street to see if folks wanted their photograph taken. My eyes lit up. I visualised myself on film wearing my new tweed coat with matching cap. I could see it recorded for all time on the photograph – not like the lovely new suit our Dickie bought me, which I ruined!

Without any hesitation I said, 'Mister, just wait here until I get my new coat and cap.' There was no way I was going to miss an opportunity such as this to be in the limelight. I raced away up the stairs like a 'lilty' and into the wardrobe where my new coat and cap were hanging. I jumped back down the stairs, three at a time, and presented myself in the hallway in front of the photographer like somebody out of Burtons shop window. 'Right Mister, take my photograph,' I commanded, standing upright with one hand in my pocket as if I was on the parade ground. The photographer made me stand in our hallway and the photograph was taken. Still wearing the coat and cap I ran into the scullery shouting, 'Hey Ma.'

As soon as she saw me she asked, 'What are you doing with that coat and cap on?'

I replied, 'There's a man at the door taking photographs and he's just taken mine.'

Ma went to the door and asked the man what he was doing; he explained he'd taken my photograph and that she owed him half a crown. 'God curse yeh, Geordie, I haven't got half a crown.' Ma gave the man a shilling. He told her he was only taking deposits today and he would collect the full payment when he delivered the photograph.

The photograph was so good Ma arranged for the man to take a full family photograph. The scene was set, everyone in their place dressed in their best clothes. I was wearing a cowboy sheriff's outfit including a Stetson hat. Even our dog 'Laddie' had been bathed for his special moment. I had a wee message to do at my Aunt Violet's across the street and on the way back I tripped and fell grazing my hands and knees. I got my jumper dirty and I was in a bit of a mess. I was in no state to have my photo taken. I cleaned myself and changed my jumper, but kept on the sheriff's outfit, gun, Stetson and all. The photograph was eventually taken and one and all looked grand.

On Monday morning I set off for my new school dressed in my tweed coat and cap. Ma took me down to Divis Street to catch the school bus. I was very excited and I couldn't wait to get my own gardening plot.

The bus took the route towards the City Centre, up Carrick Hill towards North Queen Street and along the Shore Road. Other children joined the bus along the route; it was a journey of about half-an-hour. I recall being quite shocked when I saw some of the children who got on the bus. I'd never seen anyone who was blue in colour before. There were quite a few of the children who looked blue. I later found out it was because they had a hole in their heart. There were other children who were so thin they were like bags of bones; some had humps on their backs and some children were like me, who seemed quite normal; to look at anyway, nothing seemed wrong with them. The children were all quiet on the journey to and from school; there was no diving or rushing about the bus and everyone was orderly and sat in the same seat every day.

The school was situated between the Shore Road and the Antrim Road and bordered Fort William Golf Club. The bus turned into the winding road and journeyed towards the front of the school. I saw a long wooden building in front of me with the entrance in the centre and a ramp at each side of the steps.

This was it, so up the steps and into a big long dining room we went. We were told to sit down at the benches and tables. The teachers brought out our cocoa from the kitchen situated at the far end of the room. The cocoa was just as our Dickie had told me; it was in an enamel jug and there were two platefuls of buttered bread on the table, one plate of brown bread and the other one white bread. We ate one of each with our cocoa.

Classes began. My class teacher was Mrs Cooke, a pretty lady with blonde hair. Mrs Anderson was the Head Teacher; she always wore a white coat and I thought she might have been a doctor or a nurse.

The classrooms were in another building where our academic lessons started at ten o'clock and finished at twelve noon. We had lunch between twelve noon and one o'clock and then went to another building which was known as the resting block where we had our rest period between one and two o'clock. Again, as Dickie had told me, we were allocated a bed and blanket. We all had to have a wee sleep; they were very strict about that and there hadn't to be any whispering, talking or laughing or there would be trouble.

Two or three days a week during the afternoons, if the weather was good, we would go outside to work in the garden. They gave us all a pair of wooden clogs, a fork and a spade to use. Each boy had the responsibility of keeping these gardening implements clean. It was mostly the boys that did the gardening and the girls usually did needlework. We were given a gardening plot about ten feet square and the gardener taught us where and when to plant seeds and how to put cloches over to help the seeds to grow.

Our gardens were within a walled garden that once belonged to the main house but was now the school. There were fig trees growing in the orchard and we were told not to eat the figs because they were not yet ripe. I'd had the warning but, as usual, I knew best. They looked far too tempting to leave on the tree and so I decided that I must try them, ripe or not. I devoured the figs, quite a few of them, and as with the winkles I was violently sick and everything else that comes with eating figs! My upset stomach was duly cured by the awful 'white stuff' I was administered. No beating or dysentery this time, thank goodness, just another warning not to eat un-ripened figs and do as I was told.

The pupils in my school were of mixed denominations, both Catholic and Protestant, but this was never a concern to any of us. There was never any sectarianism in those days. We always had a meal of fish on a Friday lunchtime because the Catholic children didn't eat meat on a Friday. There were eight children at each dining table – three at each side and a boy and girl at each end. They were known to us all as the 'mother' and 'father' because they were usually older and had been at the school longer. No one was allowed to leave the table until everyone had eaten up all their lunch. Meal times were not a problem to me until a plate was set in front of me on the first Friday containing white fish, creamed potatoes, green beans and carrots. The fish was covered with a thick, white, creamy sauce with green bits in it. I knew as soon as I saw the food that I didn't like it even though I hadn't tried it. I scraped at the sauce until just the fish was exposed and then began to eat the rest of the food.

The 'father', a kind boy just a few years older than me, said, 'Geordie, you will have to eat all the white sauce.'

'I don't like the white sauce and I'm not eating it,' I replied.

'You will have to eat up all of your meal because no-one is allowed to leave the table until all the food is eaten,' he explained. I still told him that I wasn't eating mine. He looked at me kindly, picked up his fork and mixed the wretched white sauce with the potato and helped me to eat my food, washing it down with a glass of milk. I tried to do the same with the help of the milk until my plate was clean. I'll never forget that boy and how he helped me that day. I dreaded the following Friday but when the fish was placed in front of me I was not deterred. This time I did manage to eat it all and future Fridays became less of a problem.

Moving around the school could be quite difficult for physically handicapped children, without the help of the abler children. We would push their wheelchairs to and from the classrooms, help them at lunchtime and assist them getting in and out of bed for their afternoon nap. The children who wore callipers would join in the games of football but needed help to get back on their feet if they fell. It made me realise how poorly some of the children were and how lucky I was. I wondered why I was at a special school; I felt good and I had no physical disabilities and I could do everything that a normal child did.

Time passed quickly and I soon became a 'father' at mealtimes. I sat in my rightful place, at long last, at the head of the table. To my right sat Freddie, a wee boy who had just started at the school. He was small and thin like me and had a little angelic face. It was his first Friday and when he started to cry I could see that, like me, he didn't like the white sauce. I immediately reflected on my own experience and said, 'Eat up your lunch, Freddie, or you won't be allowed to leave the table.' Freddie lowered his head and I could see his tears falling down his pale cheeks. Unless I did something the poor boy would have to remain at the table until he had cleared his plate. Like my 'father' had shown me, I helped him to mix the white sauce with his potatoes and wash it down with his glass of milk.

My two special friends at school were Vincie, who lived near the Falls Road, and a boy called Peter who lived in Millfield. Vincie and I liked to do the same things and, like me, there didn't seem to be anything wrong with him. He always got on the school bus at the stop before me, and Peter got on opposite his house. Peter and I sat together each morning at the front of the bus. He was a small, thin boy with dark hair and swarthy skin. He looked quite normal but was always tired and lacked energy and was not able to run around with Vincie and me. One Monday morning our school bus went sailing past Peter's house. I wasn't too worried at this because Peter had occasional absences from school when he was sick, as did lots of the children. The bus didn't stop for Peter on Tuesday or Wednesday and when it didn't stop again on Thursday I was concerned. I decided to ask the driver why he didn't stop for Peter anymore.

The driver, a small fat man replied, 'Go and sit down son.'

I asked him again, 'Why are you not stopping for Peter?' I wanted to know where Peter was because I missed him.

'Peter's not getting the bus anymore – he's dead,' the driver told me. I was stunned and stared at him, not believing his words. His gaze was not at me but straight ahead as he drove the bus towards school. 'Go and sit down now son, in case you get hurt,' he said. My hands tingled and my head felt heavy. Poor Peter, I thought, why has this happened to you; you seemed all right last Friday after school. Now I would never see my friend again. I was very sad and cried all day at school. I asked the teacher why Peter had died and she told me he had died and gone to heaven. Her kind words didn't console me and all I could do was think about my friend and stare at his empty desk. I will never forget Peter.

Chapter Five

More Heartache!

I was very sad, so was Vincie. I still had our Laddie I was very glad of that, he would always be there for me. He was given to my Ma and Da when I was born; he was only a puppy and stuck to me like glue. He grew up protecting me and always waited for me at the top of Wigton Street, by the lamp post, to meet me on my way from school.

Shortly after Peter's death I was walking home from school and some older boys were playing football in the street. The ball came over in my direction so I kicked it and it went over the spiked railings of the 'Church of God Hall'. They weren't too pleased so made me go over the railings for it. On the way back over I became impaled on the spikes. It was only my trousers, nothing too drastic but I was hanging upside down, not a pleasant experience! Laddie was licking my face and the other boys all laughed. Fortunately for me a man passing by lifted me off and saved the day.

One of the boys wasn't generous, he hit me because I had kicked the ball away.

Laddie my dog saw this and attacked the boy, biting him on his arm and drawing blood. I had to pull Laddie off him, again I went home crying.

A few days later Ma told me Laddie wasn't very well and he had to see the vet. I didn't know what a 'vet' was and she explained it was a hospital for dogs and other animals. 'It will make Laddie better,' she said. I was surprised as I didn't think there was anything wrong with him.

'What's wrong with him Ma?' I asked.

'I don't know but the vet will know,' Ma replied. She told me to take him to a neighbour's house, Walter Mack, and he would take us in his car to the vets.

For probably the first time I did as I was told, I wish I hadn't! Walter told me Laddie was ill but the vet would fix him, I was worried because I loved Laddie and wanted the best for him, so I obeyed.

It seemed a long way from Walter's house in Boundry Street to the dog hospital in Montgomery Street. We stopped outside, Laddie wouldn't budge, he just didn't want to get out of the car. He always did what I told him to do, but really didn't want to this time. 'Come on Laddie, the hospital will fix you,' I told him and reluctantly he followed me in to the vets with his head down.

Walter then tried to take Laddie away from me but Laddie growled and the more Walter pulled at the lead the worse Laddie got, baring his teeth and barking. Walter started to panic and handed the lead back to me. 'You take Laddie in the back and put him in a kennel,' Walter said.

And again reluctantly did as I was told and told Laddie again, 'Everything will be okay.' Laddie knew better and that it wasn't 'okay' but he dutifully came with me and kept putting his paws through the bars of the cage reaching out for me to hold his paw. I told him I would come and collect him the following day.

I asked Walter to bring me back to collect Laddie the following day, I continued to pester him. On the way home he took me to a sweet shop in Peter's Hill at the bottom of the Shankhill Road and bought me a Fry's Chocolate Cream bar, I suppose to try and 'shut me up'.

I had a bad feeling inside me I knew something was wrong. The following day I told my Ma I was off to Walter's house to go and collect Laddie from the vets.

It was then she dealt me the worse news any young boy wanted to hear. 'Laddie had died and was now in heaven' she told me. I was beside myself. I ran out of the house and down to Walter's house, I didn't believe her.

'Are you taking me down to get Laddie, Walter?' I pleaded. 'You promised me you would.'

'Laddie's is dead now Geordie.'

'How's he dead?'

'The vet put him to sleep,' Walter said.

'Was it because he bit the boy?'

'Yes that was part of it,' Walter replied.

It was then that I lost the plot.

'You old bastard, you told me lies, you killed my dog.' I then ran amuck, pulled his cabinet down in the house, kicked his cat up the arse, smashed his window from the outside with a brick. He tried to catch me but I was too quick. I ran away shouting, 'You old bastard you killed my fucking dog.' On my way home I also pushed a boy off his bicycle riding up our street.

Ma continued to tell me Laddie was sick; I knew he wasn't. I think they were afraid that the police would come knocking on the door and we would all be in trouble.

I ran up the stairs and went to bed, I refused to go to school the next day I told them I was sick. My poor Laddie. I still think of him and carry the guilt with me to this day, nor will I eat a Fry's Chocolate Cream bar, even now.

Chapter Six

The Young Entrepreneur

It was just me and Vincie now and we stuck together like glue at school and during the school holidays. On the Wednesday after Peter died I went to Vincie's house after school to play. Vincie was a thin boy with a mop of black hair and he was always coughing. His mummy had to slap his back several times a day to help relieve his chest. Vincie's house was similar to ours, except it had gas mantles on the walls and our house had electric lights. When I arrived at Vincie's that day I saw a lady walking away from his front door. She was dressed in a long black cloak which was draped over her head and went all the way to her shiny black shoes and she had a black veil around her face which was edged in white. I'd never seen anyone dressed like that before.

'Who is that Vincie and why is she dressed in those clothes?' I enquired.

'She's a nun Geordie, from the home,' Vincie answered.

'Is your Ma going to send you to a home then Vincie?' I asked.

'No, she's just a nun,' he replied. I still didn't understand who a nun was and what she stood for. Inside the house Vincie's Ma was sitting by a roaring fire. She was wearing a black apron with flowers on the front of it and a cardigan. His grandad was sitting opposite her and he looked very old. I thought he had been sick down the front of his waistcoat, but later found out he had spilled his food.

Vincie's Ma was crying. 'Why are you crying Ma?' Vincie asked, and I was wondering why his Ma was upset myself.

'It doesn't matter son,' she replied. Vincie kept on asking what was wrong with her. 'I've just given that nun my last half-a-crown and now I've no money to buy food for our tea. Go up to the pawn shop for me son and take your Da's shoes and brown pinstripe suit,' she said, wrapping up a pair of brown brogues in newspaper and handing them to Vincie. 'Tell the man you want half-a-crown until Saturday morning,' she instructed. Vincie and I went to the pawnshop and got half-a-crown for the shoes and five shillings for the suit. The man in the pawnshop knew me as I sometimes went there for my Aunt Violet. The pawnshop always had a musty smell because there were so many old clothes and shoes there. I used to go in holding my nose and didn't hang about long.

On our way back Vincie bought half-a-stone of potatoes, a ham shank and a cabbage as instructed by his Ma. I still couldn't understand why his Ma had given her money to the nun, especially when that was her last half-a-crown. Vincie told me that the nun always came looking for money for the church and the last time she'd come his Ma didn't have any money. I thought the nun didn't need Vincie's Ma's money as she didn't look poor and was wearing black shiny shoes. Vincie's Da wasn't best pleased either that his wife had pawned his best brogues and suit. They were having a row when we returned with the shopping. 'You're always giving them one's money – they're always crying poverty and I've told you before not to be giving them any more money,' he bawled at Vincie's Ma. I scarpered pretty sharpish, home.

'What's a nun Ma?' I asked. She explained that nuns were religious and belonged to the Roman Catholic church. They collected money from their parishioners who attended church. Ma told me that if people didn't pay up the priest would be round knocking on doors, kicking up a row if they didn't pay enough. I couldn't understand the idea of taking money from poor people. It should be the church giving money to Vincie's Ma so that she had enough to buy food.

Ma's brother, my Uncle Geordie who I was named after, married a Roman Catholic lady – Aunt Alice. I wanted to know if that made him a Roman Catholic. Ma told me that Uncle Geordie had changed his religion from Protestant to Catholic. I couldn't understand the difference but Ma told me it was far too complicated for her to start to explain and I would find out as I got older.

I might not have understood about religion but I had begun to realise that money played an important part in life. In order to make a shilling or two extra for pocket money I went round houses collecting old rags. There was a rag store at Millfield, near Brown's Square, where they accepted bundles of rags in exchange for cash. Vincie was my right-hand man in this venture and we went from door to door in our neighbourhoods with two large sacks, one for woollens and one for linens. We gratefully accepted all old clothes or rags. By the end of a day we could hardly move the sacks, but we were determined to trail our treasures along the ground to the rag store. The man in charge took our collection and placed each bag on a large weighing machine with brass weights and hooks to support the heavy sacks. He offered three shillings and sixpence for the woollens and although the sack with the linens was twice as heavy he offered only two shillings and sixpence. I knew that couldn't be right. I looked down at my big boots which were next to the bottom of the weighing machine and noticed that the rim of the man's boots was underneath the machine making it give an untrue reading.

'Mister, your fucking foot's stuck underneath the machine,' I shouted angrily, as I kicked his foot away from the scales. In turn the scales went down with a crash causing the weights at the side to fall on the ground.

'Sorry son, I didn't realise my foot was stuck underneath,' he said.

'You're a fucking liar Mister,' I shouted at him. I knew that bag was much heavier than the other one'. We eventually got five shillings for the linens. I gave Vincie the three shillings and sixpence so that he could get his dad's shoes out of the pawnshop.

Although I was only eight years old I was learning quickly just how dishonest some people could be. I learned to trust no-one, especially when it came to dealing with money.

'When are we going to collect more rags?' Vincie asked me.

'We're not collecting rags again Vincie,' I told him firmly. I'd had another idea and couldn't wait to put my plan into operation. 'We're going to collect empty beer bottles Vincie; I know where there are loads of empty bottles stacked up just waiting for us.' I told him my Aunt Susie had a huge amount all in a mound in her back yard. She always had parties at the house at weekends and there were always a lot of empty beer bottles.

Vincie and I put all the empty bottles into our hessian sacks and carried them up Boundary Street and over to Turner's Bar on the corner of Christopher Street and the Shankill Road. Turner's had a very long bar and along the back of it they had wooden barrels containing porter, sherry and ale, all in a long line. Each barrel had a brass tap in the middle so that the drink could be poured directly into the customers drinking glasses. The bar was highly decorative and had unusual stuffed animals displayed all around. There were stuffed lion's heads, a rhino's head, wild buffalo and a sheep with six legs – all in a glass case. On the walls were African spears and shields. Vincie and I had hundreds of empty bottles and it took us four trips from Aunt Susie's to take them to the bar. The man behind the bar who was dressed in a white apron, black waistcoat and black tie counted all the bottles. 'You've got five shillings worth here,' he told us. I knew that was rubbish. I knew we should get a halfpenny per bottle and I had counted to at least eight shillings before I lost count of the number of bottles we had.

'Mister, are you sure you have counted all those bottles we brought you?' I asked.

'Yes,' he replied. 'That's all you're getting – five shillings,' and he gave us two shillings and sixpence each.

'You're a fucking liar Mister,' I shouted.

'Come here you wee bastard,' he replied as he let on to run at us. We ran out into the street but he couldn't catch us 'cos he had a big fat belly.

'Leave it Geordie, let's go,' Vincie said.

'No, fuck him, he's robbed us and I'm going back in to tell him he's a fucking robber,' I replied. I returned on my own to the bar; there was no-one about. I lifted one of the spears from the wall behind the bar and shouted, 'you're a fucking robber Mister,' and I threw the spear with my full force like a true African warrior. It went hurtling through the air, across the bar and right into one of the oak barrels. I scarpered and never returned.

Our Wee Geordie with Cousin Brenda and Big Sister Isobel

Chapter Seven

Gungadin!

Although the war years were over for more than eight years by now, little boys like us, who had been born just after the war, liked to discuss our fathers' heroic war years. My friends and I would meet up in each other's front porch and talk all about those days, reliving each battle as if we had encountered every manoeuvre. We would dress up in our fathers' old uniforms, helmets, tunics and trousers, carrying their water bottles and gas masks. We even wore their big black leather army boots which weighed an absolute ton.

One of our group was nicknamed Gunga – we called him that after Gungadin the famous Indian water carrier. His father was in the Parachute Regiment and Gunga had boasted that his father had a real parachute stored up in the attic of his house. We decided it would be good idea to relive Gunga's Da's live jump onto German territory with the use of the real parachute. Gunga's house was in Percy Street where the houses were three stories high – a good height for the jump. Five of my friends, together with Gunga and I, ran up all the stairs and climbed into the attic. Gunga put on his Da's uniform, helmet and all, and we strapped the parachute on his back. We were all dressed in our Da's uniforms looking like the real 'Da's army'. Everyone was excited about the jump and our only disappointment was the fact that we did not have real rifles! We heaved the sash window out of the frame and Gunga climbed out onto the slopping slate roof outside the window. We had all watched and loved old war films and we wanted Gunga's maiden jump to be as authentic as possible. We had watched as each soldier was tapped on the back before he jumped from the aircraft. When Gunga was ready he too was tapped on the back. 'Jump Gunga, jump,' we commanded, and without hesitation Gunga leapt from the high slopping roof into mid-air clutching the parachute rip cord. The poor boy unexpectedly dropped like a lead weight directly to the ground where the flagstones awaited him. We all watched with horror from the window, astonished that the parachute didn't open. Gunga had hit the ground and was lying motionless. 'He's forgotten to pull the string,' someone yelled, and with that we all made a dash for the stairs as fast as we could, each one trying to push past the other on the narrow steep stairs.

Luckily for Gunga he had landed on the parachute pack which was heavier than him and must have broken his fall. However, when we reached the street we found him unconscious and we began slapping his face, telling him to wake up. 'You forgot to pull the string. If you'd pulled the string you'd be alright,' someone shouted. He had a broken leg and wrist and was taken by ambulance to hospital. Poor Gunga – if only he'd pulled the string!

I made my way home, still in full battle dress and thinking what a shame it was that Gunga's parachute hadn't opened. I told Ma about the escapade but she wasn't best pleased and I was given a walloping for my stupidity. The good news was that Gunga survived his jump and duly arrived home with one leg in plaster and looking like he had just returned wounded from battle! As the saying goes, 'You're a better man than I am Gungadin'!

Chapter Eight

Country House Life

All my summer holidays and weekends from the age of about six or seven years were spent at our country house. Now, when you think of a country house you may think of a large dwelling set in the grounds of a country estate, and maybe the owners titled Lord and Lady. Well, not so here. Our dear country house was small with the exterior fully whitewashed. It was a pretty place and I had some wonderful days there. We would set off, usually Ma, Da and our Sammy and Alec. We would get off the green bus at the Temple Crossroads near Ballynahinch. I loved the countryside and it kept me away from trouble back home.

When we arrived we all had our own jobs to do. I was in charge of the dry toilet and getting water from the well. I had to take the dry toilet, which was a bucket, down the fields, dig a big hole and bury the contents, replacing the soil with the grass sods on the top. I didn't really like this job at all but I carried out the task willingly. I didn't mind collecting water from the well but I had to do it several times each day. Ma had bought two lovely new white enamel buckets, and instead of taking them one at a time to the well I thought I would save a journey by carrying them both on a long stick. However, the buckets kept slipping off as there were no notches to stop them. On reaching the well I climbed down the moss-covered stone steps. The water level was high on this particular day – almost level with the bottom step. I lowered both buckets, one in each hand, into the water, but as they started to fill they became so heavy that my hobnail boots slipped off the bottom step and dragged me into the water. My only thoughts were about the new buckets Ma had just bought. I knew I better not let go of the handles and risk losing them in the deep water. I was totally shocked and the water was icy cold and the buckets had filled and were slowly pulling me down.

I don't know how I did it, but my boots that had originally made me slip came to my rescue when I managed to wedge them at each side of the stone well. I kept one bucket wedged between one leg and the wall of the well and the other bucket between both legs. Both buckets ended up empty as I threw them one at a time over my head and then managed to rescue myself from the deep cold water. I eventually managed to half fill both buckets and made my way back less than pleased with the wretched well. I was soaking wet and crying by the time I reached our house.

'What happened to you wee son?' Ma asked.

'I nearly drowned in that fucking well,' I cried.

Da asked me why I didn't let go of the buckets and I told him it was because Ma had only just bought them new. From then on Da got the water from the well! It was a good outdoor life for a wee buck like me compared to the back streets in Belfast. I loved to help at

Robinson's farm, taking the cows in to be milked and helping Ma bake soda and potato bread. Da let me help him in the plot where he grew vegetables - beetroot, scallions, horseradish and lots more. These were great days!

The next military operation with my friends was at the country house. The advanced expedition forces were en route on the green bus from Ormeau Avenue, Belfast, to the Temple Crossroads! There were six of us including Billie Leslie, Tom Mills and Matt Thompson. We trudged from the crossroads on the two-mile walk to the white-washed cottage with the red door. This was where our Jim and Ruby spent their honeymoon. We all had rucksacks with provisions, including several bars of chocolate. When we arrived I detailed the troops about their different tasks – lighting the old range, chopping sticks, emptying the dry toilet and collecting the water. These were not to be my tasks on this visit! As a leader of a platoon I had to delegate. I was about nine, probably the eldest of us all and the most streetwise; you could say I was nine going on twenty-nine. I was influenced greatly by my elder brothers and was subsequently given a long rein by my parents, as they knew I could take care of myself quite adequately.

We cooked our tea of sausage, brown free-range eggs and the compulsory baked beans and potato bread. We had been out and had collected sticklebacks and frogs and put them in jam jars. One lad told us that during the war years his Da had eaten frog's legs; we contemplated his, together with snails, for starters but then gave it a miss! Cooking wasn't alien to me, even at nine years old. Our Sammy, after one of his late nights out used to love his Ulster fry the following morning. I would cook him his fry of egg, bacon, sausage, tomato, soda and potato bread, accompanied with several rounds of hot buttered toast. He gave me two shillings for my trouble but sometimes if I held out he would give me a half crown. He could be real lazy sometimes; if the fire needed stoking he couldn't be bothered his arse to get off the sofa and do it himself, so I didn't think a half crown was too much to ask.

Later, when it was dark outside, we settled down in front of the fire. With just six young boys alone in the country, it wasn't long before ghost stories were being told. The hairs on the back of our necks were standing up and some of the boys were afraid to go out to the toilet. I persuaded them there was nothing to be afraid of and we all went out as a team.

One boy, who was only about eight years old, cried and wanted to go home. 'Please Geordie, get me home, get me home,' he pleaded. Unable to persuade him to stay I agreed to take him back to the bus stop. With the light of a hurricane lamp we both marched the two miles to the crossroads.

When the number sixty-five bus came I said to the driver, 'This boy's afraid, will you let him off at Ormeau Avenue? He wants to go home to his Ma.' I started to make my way back to the cottage alone. It was really dark and it was now raining and windy. Half way back the lamp went out – blown out or out of oil I thought. The ghost stories now became real to me and I began to run in the pitch darkness. I was relieved to arrive back at the cottage that night! The following days were spent with my pals dangling from the knotted rope that swung out over the stream. Our challenge was to drop off the rope onto the far bank without getting wet. Needless to say there were many wet wee bucks after this challenge. Collecting frogs and toads and playing games such as hide and seek were our other favourite pursuits. This was always a favourite game as there were so many good places to hide; up trees and in the undergrowth, coming out stinking and never washing. Washing ourselves was never very high on our agenda, at least not on that weekend.

We all trudged back wearily to the crossroads to catch the last bus back to Belfast on that Sunday night. We all must have looked as black as the miners used to do when they were returning from the coalface.

Chapter Nine

Colwyn Bay, Wales

Like my brothers Alex and Sammy before me, I wanted to join the Boy Scouts. When I was eleven or twelve years old I joined the Twentieth Scout Troop in Wood Vale Road. My most memorable trip with the Scouts was on the Belfast to Liverpool overnight Steam Ship crossing. I'll tell you why.

She was about sixteen or seventeen years old. She asked me my name and where I lived. She was good looking and her name was Virginia. She started to kiss me. 'Do you want to go for a walk Geordie, up on the top deck?' she quietly asked me. I could feel her warm breath on my ear and she smelt just lovely. Her hair was dark and her lips were red. She led me by the hand up the steps; she felt so soft and nice. 'Come on, we'll sit down here,' Virginia said, as she pushed me down next to her onto the bench-style seat. We sat together and talked, then we put our arms around each other. This was all new to me but I liked it very much. I think she must have done this before as she seemed to know what she was doing. Again she kissed me with her big red warm lips. I felt her hand on my bare knee – I was still wearing short trousers. 'Come on, let's get underneath the bench so we can lie down,' Virginia said, breathing heavily as if she was out of breath. She kissed me more passionately as we lay together underneath the bench. It was a secluded place and no one knew we were there. Her tongue was pushed between my lips and entered my mouth and she placed my hand underneath her bra so that I could take out one of her tits. It felt soft, warm and wobbly as I squeezed it. She was moving around quite a lot and she opened up her legs to me, so I put my hand inside her knickers and played around down there for a while. I remember thinking it felt a bit like a piece of my Da's wire wool. It was wet and she moved my hand up and down her fanny. I don't remember having any sexy feelings but I suppose I must have done. She was writhing and groaning. I thought at first there was something wrong with her. She kissed me even more and more until her groaning became very loud, then she suddenly stopped and pushed my hand away. I thought I'd upset her and it wasn't long before she got up and left. I never saw her again. She certainly knew what she wanted that night and that was my first experience of girls and sex! Wow!

I thought Virginia was nice and I enjoyed the closeness and softness of a girl, but I didn't really get anything out of the experience that night. It obviously made me hungry, as my next move was to buy a tuna sandwich, or was it fish paste, can't really remember, from the boat's kiosk.

I tried to eat the sandwich but the taste and smell of it just wasn't that great so I told the man who sold it to me. I held out the sandwich with my right hand, 'Mister, smell this sandwich, do you think it smells funny?'

'It does indeed son,' he agreed as he opened another packet and they smelt fine. I ate my new sandwich using my left hand and it certainly smelt a lot sweeter. It was only when I put my other hand up to my face I thought I should have made sure my hands were washed before eating my tuna sandwich!

My trip with the Scouts was a most memorable time, in more ways than one, and it was the first time away from home without Ma and Da. Our destination was Colwyn Bay in North Wales. The campsite had several tents in a large field with a wooden toilet and wash block. There were scout troops from all over the UK and each troop had a leader who would set us daily tasks, such as knots, campfire building and cooking. One of the leaders was a small man about fifty years old with grey hair. He appeared to take an unusual interest in me and he invited my leader and me to his home for tea. No other boy was invited, just me, and I wondered why. I arrived at the big detached house overlooking Colwyn Bay. It was very posh and smelt of polish and mothballs. A lady came into the drawing room and she put her arm around me and started to cry. 'Hello George,' she sobbed, and I wondered what I had done or why this lovely lady, who I had never met before, was crying and holding me in her arms.

I noticed a photograph on the mantelpiece of a small boy about my age, dressed in a Scout's uniform. I thought it was me. 'Missus, why have you got a photograph of me on your mantelpiece?' I asked.

She started to cry again. 'That's my son Robert, he was killed a year ago on his bicycle and he looks just like you, doesn't he?' I could see that he did. The lady looked very sad and kept her eyes on me the whole time I was there. I'd never been to such a posh place and to be honest I was enjoying the attention. We had a lovely tea, with silver knives and forks and real china teacups. The tea was poured from the silver teapot – a posh afternoon for a wee boy from the back streets of Belfast.

Before we left their house that day I remember the man and lady asking me if I would like them to visit me back in Northern Ireland. I was never worried or concerned that Ma would have sent me away to live with these people but I have wondered what my destiny may have been like had I have done so.

I was growing up fast and learning about life very quickly. Although my education at school was limited I was sharp and pretty quick on the uptake.

Ma and Da always thought it important I attend church and Sunday school. I looked forward to Sundays and attending St Luke's Parish Church in Northumberland Street. After prayers all us youngsters would play on the huge granite stones surrounding the church. We would pretend it was the castle battlements and run ragged trying to defend the castle walls from the imminent invaders.

Our Isobel married Jackie at St Luke's, which is the Church of Ireland. When I reached the appropriate age I attended weekly for my confirmation classes. It was there I learned to recite the books of the Old and New Testaments, which I can still recite to this very day, as well as the Catechism.

I left my special school a healthy enough wee lad; I survived, many didn't. I was one of the lucky ones, much to Ma and Da's delight. I now attended the Senior Public Elementary school in Hemsworth Square which was a bus journey and then about a one mile walk from the bus destination to the school.

School started promptly at nine o'clock but I never arrived until five past nine. The bus couldn't get me there any earlier; I was always five minutes late. I regularly got six slaps on each hand for being late, however that didn't worry me as six slaps was nothing. After about three weeks the headmaster asked me why I persisted being late. I told him the only bus I could get to school got me there after school started and there was nothing I could do about it. I knew he felt bad about the canings. 'Why didn't you tell me this George?' he enquired. I couldn't have told him; after all he was the headmaster! He used to get me to do all his messages and didn't seem to mind me being late after that.

It was August now and I had been back home from Scout camp for about one month. When I arrived in our street one day, my eyes lit on a gleaming Sunbeam Rapier motorcar with its hood down parked outside our house. Inside the house the man and lady from Colwyn Bay were having tea with my Ma. They kept their promise to visit me at home and they were staying at the Grand Central Hotel in Royal Avenue in Belfast – a very posh hotel. They had come a long way just for tea.

They were all sitting talking when Ma asked, 'Son, Mr and Mrs Jones would like you to go and live with them in Wales, would you like that?'

'Why would I want to live with these people?' I asked.

'They would like to adopt you son, to look after you because you look like their son who was killed,' Ma answered.

There was never any doubt in my mind that I would not be going to live in Wales – 'No,' I answered crossly, 'I'd miss you all.' The lady looked sad so I said no more. Colwyn Bay was all right for a Scout camp, but I didn't want to leave my family and everything I had ever known.

Our Alex and Sammy heard Ma telling my Da about how the people wanted to adopt me. 'Go on Ma, sell him, give him away, he's a bloody wee nuisance' they laughed, but I wasn't laughing. I started to tell people my Ma was trying to sell me.

She was angry at that and gave me a good shaking, saying, 'I'm not trying to sell you wee son. I wouldn't sell you for all the money in the world.'

For quite a while afterwards my parents got letters from the lady and gentleman. Alex and Sammy told Ma she should have sold me while she had the chance! I never saw or heard from them again but I could understand how awful it was for them to lose their only son.

Chapter Ten

The Reluctant Builder

Monday morning arrived and I set off for Jimmy Graham's Building Contractors at New Barnsley Estate on Springfield Road in Belfast. I went with our Alex and Sammy. On the way we picked up my brother-in-law Jackie who was married to our Isobel.

Stevenson and Turner and hairdressing were in the past. This was the building game and it was natural, I suppose, for me to eventually end up there as the apprentice bricklayer to my brothers and Jackie who were men known as the finest 'brickies' in the Belfast area. Right from the start our Sammy told me, 'Listen wee lad, you're not just gonna be a bricklayer, you're gonna be a master bricklayer, and one day you just might be as good as us.' I was a determined young man and wanted to be the best at what I did. During lunch and tea breaks I spent my time in the engineer's office learning to read drawings and levels for setting out building sites. I gained experience by moving from site to site, building various projects until, during the early 1960s, the building industry in Northern Ireland took a sharp decline. After 9 months in the job Graham's went bankrupt which meant we were all out of work. My brothers and Jackie left Northern Ireland to work in America, but I couldn't go with them as I was only 18.

I managed to get a job at F T Ferguson's at Carnmoney as an apprentice bricklayer. By chance I met the owner, Jimmy Ferguson, who asked me what experience I had. I told him I had three years' experience and mentioned various sites I'd worked on. 'Do you know how to build manholes?' he asked me.

'I'm an expert at manholes Mr Ferguson,' I lied. In fact, I'd never even seen a manhole until now as I gazed horrified down a huge hole in the road. There were pipes around two inches in diameter sticking out into the hole from every direction. Mr Ferguson told me he wanted me to build it in 9-inch manhole bond. My heart sank and I thought, holy shit, how the fuck am I going to get out of this?

'Are you happy with that now young fella; are you sure you can do it?' Mr Ferguson enquired.

Taking my tools, I climbed down into the hole. I hadn't a notion how to start. I'd learned all about English Garden wall bond, Flemish Bond, Old English Bond and even Monks diagonal bond, which very few people would have known about, but what the fuck a 9-inch manhole bond was, I hadn't a clue.

I sat on my toolbox thinking and looking at the pipes. Suddenly, inspiration gripped me. Why not go and see how the other manholes are built! Learning from these I built the manhole, over six feet high, within three days – which was good going, considering I had no labourer to help me. Mr Ferguson inspected my work and congratulated me. 'When you have this manhole finished Geordie,' he said, 'how do you propose to get out of it? You won't always have a ladder.' I realized then he'd given me galvanised step irons to put into the walls but it hadn't even dawned on me what they were for. It took me just as long to put the step irons into the walls as it had taken me to build the manhole. I soon became a real expert at manholes. All I built during the next six months was fucking manholes. However, I became a competent builder and later even worked building Mr Ferguson's own house.

It was a really wet day and I was patching up windowsills at a house in the Ferndale development, working with DPC felt. Unluckily for me a piece of the felt hit me and penetrated my left eye. The pain was excruciating and I couldn't see anything from my left eye. I knew it was bad news and I went immediately to the Royal Victoria Hospital ENT department on the Falls Road. After being examined by doctor a nurse came and told me to get undressed and put on a dressing gown. She told me I was being admitted to hospital. I told her I couldn't do that as my Ma and Da would be expecting me home. There was a public phone box across the road from our house and people passing by would lift the receiver if they heard the phone ring. I managed to get someone to take the message across to Ma and she and Da and our Albert came to see me. For the next two weeks I had to lie still on my back. The Professor Mr McEwan said there was a possibility that I could lose my sight in the injured eye. I couldn't believe what he was saying and I cried a lot. I received treatment three times a day to the eye that was completely bandaged so that no light would enter. The bandages were removed after about one week and I was able to detect light and shadows, but I couldn't recognise people. Gradually my sight improved and it was decided that my eye would not need to be removed.

My two weeks in hospital was to change my life, although I didn't know that then. It was January 1965 and I was eighteen years old. While lying on my back I was dependent on the nursing staff to care for me. On my very first day in hospital I met a very attractive blonde-haired nurse. She was a well-made girl, I noticed. She was very kind, older than me and had a friendly smile and a reassuring presence. I felt attracted to her from the start. 'Nurse Harbinson, I need to do a wee; I haven't been for days,' I told her.

'You have to use the bed bottle George,' she replied. I was really asking her if I could get up and go to the toilet but I knew I wouldn't be allowed.

'It's difficult for me to use it; I feel I'm wetting the bed,' I told her. She ran the cold water in the hand basin next to my bed and placed her hand underneath the running water. Then she placed her cold hand on to my tummy. That certainly did the trick. 'Nurse Harbinson, you had better get me another bottle.' I filled the second bottle as well. I was very grateful to her and from that moment on our relationship took on a new meaning. I couldn't wait for her to start her shifts on my ward and felt I wanted to see her and be near her more and more.

These were feelings I'd never experienced before. I'd had a couple of girlfriends who I'd kissed, but that's all. I'd never had a sexual relationship. At that time I was friendly with two girls, Vickie Simmons, she was well-made as well, and my steady girlfriend, Valerie Kinch, who was not so well-made! They were both nice girls but I never had the feelings for them that I had for Nurse Harbinson. I was disappointed when Nurse Harbinson told me she was going off duty for the next two days. Another well-made nurse, Christine Lanes cared for me. She looked after me well but wasn't a patch on Nurse Harbinson; I couldn't wait for her to return to duty. I was overjoyed when she returned to night duty.

'How's my favourite patient?' she whispered.

'I'm feeling much better now that you're here,' I replied.

'I bet you tell all the nurses that George,' she said.

'No, no, just you Nurse Harbinson.' I smiled at her.

At about 11pm when I still couldn't sleep, Matron accompanied Nurse Harbinson on their ward rounds. I told them I couldn't sleep and when Matron had left the ward Nurse Harbinson returned to my bedside.

She shone the torch into my eyes and said, 'Are you still not sleeping George?' She sat down beside me and I asked her if I could hold her hand. 'Of course you can,' was her reply.

'Can I give you a kiss as well?' I asked her.

'Of course you can,' she replied again. I was so surprised she agreed, so I gave her a wee peck on the lips. It was very nice and I realised my feelings for her were growing.

During my last week in hospital we became more and more friendly. On her last night on duty we went together into an empty sideward. I kissed her more passionately and placed my arms around her. I was very aroused. She was worried we would be caught as it was against all ethics for nurses to be involved with their patients. I told her there and then I wanted to make love to her, but carried on to tell her I couldn't. 'Why not George?' she asked.

'I'm going out with another girl at the moment and it wouldn't be fair to her,' I replied. But that wasn't the real reason, only a very small part of it. The truth of the matter was I didn't know how to make love; I'd never done it before. We stayed in the sideward a while longer, kissing and hugging. She asked me if I'd like to meet her off duty and gave me her home telephone number. That was just the beginning.

Wee Geordie's dad Albert in Burmah 1945 with pet monkey

Chapter Eleven

My First Love

After I was discharged from hospital I telephoned Anne and asked if I could see her again. She invited me to her home in Orby Drive. It was a lot grander than my home. It was a very nice semi-detached house. I remember the day well. Her Da was upstairs in bed as he worked for Harland and Wolff the shipbuilders and was on night shift. Anne wore a black polo neck sweater with a string of pearls around her neck. She looked very elegant and I felt very happy to be with her again. I'm sure I also looked very well as I was wearing my best navy blue suit and white shirt. We had a cup of coffee together and talked the whole afternoon. She told me she was the secretary of the nurses Christian Fellowship at the Royal Victoria Hospital and then continued to tell me about her family. She was the eldest daughter of Bob Harbinson and had two sisters and a young brother.

Anne's father and her mother had split up when Anne was only nine years old. Their mother put Anne and her siblings into a taxi and the taxi driver was told to take them to their grandfather's house in Orby Drive. That was the last time they ever saw their mother. She had met a man who was a bricklayer the same as me and had left Anne's father with the children. I could never understand how a mother could ever leave four children behind and never see them again. Anne and her brother and sisters were brought up by their father, grandfather, grandmother and aunts who all lived at Orby Drive.

I realised that afternoon I had fallen in love with her and wanted to see her more and more. She went back to work after her days off and from that day on we saw each other every single day.

When Anne was working she lived at the nurse's home, Bostock House, which was very close to the hospital. After I finished work I travelled by bus to Bostock House to see her. Anne had her own room there, but rules were strict and friends were not allowed in the bedrooms. We were very fortunate in that the lady in charge used to reserve one of two reception room, and so we always had our privacy to spend special time together and talk.

My bus fare to see Anne cost me seven old pence. My wages as a bricklayer were £2.10 for a fifty-hour week. I never told Anne that I only had enough money for a one-way bus ticket. When I left her in the evenings she would watch me from her bedroom window. I walked across the Falls Road where I waited until the bus came and we would blow each other kisses and wave goodbye. I always got on the bus, but what she didn't know was that I got off at the next stop and pretended to the bus conductor I'd got on the wrong bus.

The conductor got to know me after a few months and enquired why I only stayed on for one stop. 'I'm on the wrong bus,' I told him unconvincingly.

'You can't be on the wrong bus lad, this is the last bus to Belfast and the Whitewell terminus,' he smiled. I lived near the Whitewell terminus so I had to come clean and admitted I'd no money for the fare. Each night when Anne was on the late shift I did this, never letting her know I didn't have the money. It was about eight miles to walk home but it certainly came as a great relief that on this night I could stay on the bus all the way home. I felt proud when I actually had the money to pay the fare, but sometimes the conductor gave me a nod and a wink and I got a free ride home. That's love for you!

One wet Friday night in February 1965 I asked Anne if she would marry me. We had been to the Ritz cinema to see The Sound of Music. I'd walked her back to the nurse's home after eating fish and chips on the way. We were standing at the back of the Maternity Unit in the hospital grounds. 'Anne, I've something to ask you,' I said hurriedly. It seemed ages before she spoke, as if she knew what I was going to say. 'Will you marry me Anne?' I asked her as I held her gaze.

'Why do you want to marry me?' she replied.

'Because I love you and want to spend the rest of my life with you,' I answered.

'How do you know you are in love with me George?' she asked.

'Because I want to be with you every day,' I said.

'Is it not because you are infatuated with me?' she enquired. I didn't know what she meant, so I asked her. 'Because I was your nurse, George. How could you support me? Where would we live? You are only an apprentice bricklayer and you don't earn a lot of money.'

'One day I'll own my own business and I'll build you a house,' I enthused.

'What would you say if I said yes?' she asked.

'It would make me the happiest fella in the world,' I replied excitedly. 'We would get married in two years' time Anne, what do you say?'

'Will we get engaged first?' she asked. I told her we would. 'Yes George, I will marry you,' she agreed. I started shouting and dancing with happiness. I couldn't believe Anne had agreed to marry me. I was the happiest fella in the world. 'You will have to come and meet my father and my aunts, but we won't tell them anything about this just yet.'

Two weeks before Easter that year I met Anne's father and her two aunts. I was on my best behaviour, but that didn't really matter because they didn't like me. I wasn't welcomed at all at that first meeting and her Aunt Nell described me as 'the devil'. They had only met me once over a cup of tea; they didn't even know me. I suppose it was because of my background and the glaring fact I was a bricklayer, with no prospects for Bob Harbinson's eldest daughter. Perhaps if I'd been a doctor I would have been more happily received. Anne had been dating a doctor from the hospital when I met her and I suppose her family must have thought he was more suitable than just an apprentice bricklayer.

Anne's family were enthusiastic Christian churchgoers and their opinion also greatly influenced Anne. A week prior to Easter 1965 Anne decided it would be best if we didn't see each other anymore. I was greatly upset, deeply hurt and had a sense of loss within me. We parted company and shook hands sadly. I felt empty and wondered what the future would hold for me now. Apart from Anne and I being together and our plans for the future I had no other purpose to my life. I missed her terribly and all I could so was think of her constantly.

I carried on with my building work at the new Rothmans Carreras factory in Greenisland but I had no happiness in my life. We had both talked about going to Portrush, a seaside town on the beautiful North Antrim Coast about 60 miles from Belfast, for the Easter holiday. Even though Anne and I were not seeing each other, I decided to go anyway with some of my mates, secretly hoping that I would bump into Anne who was going with some of her nursing friends. Easter came and we boarded the train aptly named The Portrush Flyer. I was wearing my brand new Aran sweater which had cost me five quid even then. It could be very cold along the North Coast, especially at Easter. There were four of us travelling with one tent which we pitched near to the Royal Portrush Golf Course. I was totally preoccupied looking for Anne that weekend, and all four of us walked around with Anne in mind. I eventually saw her on the Sunday afternoon walking up the main street. My stomach turned over and a thrill went through my body. I had longed to see her again. Lots of things went through my mind. What would she say? Would she ignore me? More importantly, what was I going to say to her? She was wearing a lemon sweater and an anorak and a headscarf that I had bought for her.

Compared to us boys who were all quite rough and ready, the girls were very posh. Anne and I just looked at each other.

'Hello George,' Anne said.

'Hello Anne,' I replied. I felt nervous but hoped she wouldn't notice. Her friends and my mates walked on and left us talking. We talked politely and then she took my hand.

'I've missed you George, very much,' she said.

'I've missed you too. It's a pity your dad and aunts don't like me.'

'Their opinions aren't important any more. It's what you and I feel about each other that matters now,' she said.

'If we see each other again you will only get into more trouble,' I stated. I didn't want her to have any more problems with her family because of me.

'Let me deal with that,' she said.

I didn't argue. I just asked her when I could see her. 'Is tonight too soon?' she asked. I felt so happy again.

'No, of course it's not too soon.' I couldn't hide my feelings so I just hugged and kissed her in the middle of the main street.

Romantically, we arranged to meet in the fish and chip shop! We ordered tea, bread and butter and talked about the future we had previously planned. Where we would live, when we would marry and how many children we were going to have. Afterwards we walked along the beach on a cold but dry night. I was the happiest fella in the whole world.

We walked along the coast to where the tent was. I made her a cup of tea on our little stove and we ate some chocolate biscuits sitting outside the tent until it was dark. I asked Anne if she wanted to stay the night.

'Where will I sleep?' she asked me.

'Right beside me at the top end of the tent,' I told her. I just wanted to hold her near me. She wasn't getting away from me again!

'It wouldn't be right to do this to your friends,' she insisted, but I assured her they wouldn't mind.

By the time my mates arrived back Anne and I were snug in my sleeping bag. This was the first time I had slept the whole night long with a girl and it felt wonderful. We kissed and cuddled each other, but nothing more; it was a lovely night. I didn't sleep very much; my thoughts were full of our future together. I knew then I was going to marry Anne and nothing or no-one was going to stand in my way. I knew my life was going to change for the better and that this would bring new responsibilities.

We got up about 6.00am the following morning and tiptoed out of the tent past my mates, who hadn't even seen the two of us. I walked Anne back to her boarding house in Atlantic Avenue and arranged to meet again later that evening. Easter had, all in all, turned out pretty good.

Pit stop on the Road on the way to Portrush at Water Foot, to raise money for Cancer Foundation

Chapter Twelve

Geordie Meets the Family

Anne and I saw each other every evening, even when she worked late shifts and night duties. She had just passed her nursing examinations and was now a fully qualified staff nurse at the Royal Victoria Hospital. She was a very dedicated nurse and her patients were her first priority. I would wait at the nurse's home until she finished her late shift at 8.30pm, sometimes she was late and I would get very impatient because I wanted to see her so much. I would occasionally write her notes telling her I couldn't wait any longer, but I never did leave. I ended up giving her the note I'd written when she eventually turned up. She would explain to me that her patients were ill people and they came first and that I would have to learn to be more patient. That was the first lesson Anne taught me, patience. That was a word I knew little about.

We still hadn't told Anne's family about our future plans and we were unsure how they would react. We decided that I would start to go to church with Anne and her family on Sundays. It would be a way of them getting to know me better. They attended Orange Field

Presbyterian Church and they went twice each Sunday. They hadn't far to go as they lived next door to the church. Anne's Aunt Lila played the organ and her Aunt Nell and her father Bob were both elders of the church. Anne was a Sunday school teacher.

My first invitation to join them for Sunday lunch was most memorable. We had been to morning service and I had dressed smartly for the occasion. Everyone had their own place at the table which was in the back room of the large semi-detached house. I sat between Anne and Bob. I recall that the table was very nicely set with beautiful china and fancy knives and forks with bone handles. I reflected on the grand tea I'd had when I was just a boy in Colwyn Bay. I thought I was on my best behaviour. My soup was set down before me and I thought that was an indication to get stuck in straight away. I began to enjoy the soup unaware that no one else had started to eat when I felt Anne nudge my leg. 'George, we have to say grace first,' Anne whispered. By this time I'd had about four spoonfuls of soup. I put my spoon down on the clean white Irish Linen tablecloth leaving a large wet stain – my second mistake. It was really tasty soup and I couldn't wait to get grace over with. I seemed to be the only one who was enjoying it as I was making the most noise and had finished long before anyone else and then requested a second bowl. Roast beef followed, accompanied by boiled potatoes in their jackets with peas and carrots. I'd never eaten potatoes boiled in their jackets before, so I watched the others to see how they ate theirs. Everyone stuck their fork into the potato bowl, which had been placed majestically in the centre of the table and peeled the brown skin away from the white fluffy insides, placing the skin on their side plate. This looked easy so I plunged my fork into the biggest potato left in the bowl. As I attempted to peel it, half of the potato fell in small pieces on the tablecloth while the other half hit the leg of my chair and disintegrated on the carpet. Needless to say I was totally embarrassed but managed to get through the rest of the meal without further mishap. Surprisingly enough I was even invited back.

The Sunday schedule at the Harbinson household was church at 11.30am followed by lunch and Sunday school in the afternoon. I would wait for Anne at the house while she took her Sunday school class and then we would have tea before attending evening service at 7.00pm. We always returned to the house for supper of tea with home baked scones, boiled cake and biscuits. They kept a good table did the Harbinson's. Bob always ran us back to Bostock House on Sunday evenings and this became my normal Sunday when Anne was off duty.

My Ma and Da were happy that I'd met a girl like Anne. 'Anne's a lady,' Ma would say. 'Our wee Geordie's met a lady.' Ma was very pleased and became very fond of Anne.

My outspoken brother Dickie used to say, 'Why are you going with a girl who is older than you and not as good looking as Vickie Simmons or Valerie Kinch?' He was of course referring to my first two girlfriends who were the same age as me, but now that I was older I could talk back to him.

'Mind your own business; it's got nothing to do with you anyway. I'm going to marry Anne.'

'You're mad, wee lad. You could get any girl you want, you're the best looking fella in this whole area,' he replied.

My brothers were all married now and Isabel was married to Jackie. Everything seemed to be going well. Anne and I were so happy together and her family seemed to be accepting me more as time passed. I hadn't yet taken Anne to my home because I was ashamed that I lived in a council house. She had met my Ma, Dickie and his wife Sally in the town. Sadly, Anne never met my Da.

It was on 13 November 1965. Anne and I had just finished an evening meal in the Cotter's Kitchen restaurant in Adelaide Street in Belfast and had walked back to the nurse's home. On our arrival there a message was waiting for me at the reception desk that I had to go home immediately as there had been an accident. Luckily I had enough money that night for my journey home by bus. That journey seemed the longest I had ever endured. During the thirty-five-minute journey I kept praying, over and over again, 'Please God, don't let anything happen to my Ma and Da.' I had a feeling the news at home wasn't going to be good.

When I had said my farewells to Ma and Da that morning as they set off on the journey to Dublin with Isabel and Jackie, my Da had called over to me, 'Geordie, make sure you look after yourself.' I remember those words clearly.

'Yes, I will Da. Have a good time in Dublin,' I had shouted as the car pulled away with Jackie at the wheel. That was the last time I saw my Da alive.

My brother Jim's wife, Ruby, and Sally sat me down and told me the bad news. There had been a terrible accident just outside Dundalk and my Da had been killed. Jackie's car had broken down on the way home. It was a dark November night and they were pushing the car into the roadside. My Da had moved Isobel from the rear off-side of the car telling her that the drivers in that area were not very good and that it was too dangerous for her to be near the other cars. He took her place and a car coming from behind crashed into Da, killing him outright and severing his legs. Jackie was never to drive a car again, after that fateful night.

I was nineteen at the time of Da's death and I missed him greatly. A large part of my life was missing - we were very close. I remembered his last words to me and I have been taking care ever since. A kind man who lived across the street drove Anne and I to Dundalk that night. I wanted to see my Da and say my farewells. My thoughts were of his life and how he had fought bare-fisted down the Chapel fields so that he could feed his large family. I thought of how he had been part of the 'forgotten army' fighting the Japanese in the jungles of Burma and now felt angry that he had met an untimely death at the hands of a drunken driver. It didn't seem fair.

Da's funeral was one of the biggest Belfast had ever seen. There were hundreds of wreaths and over one thousand people from all religions and all walks of life paid their respects. It was such a cold day the piper could barely play and the bugler was unable to play the 'last post'. It was a sad but proud day for me.

Chapter Thirteen

The Show- Off

It wasn't long after Da died that Isobel and Jackie went to live in America. Ma's heart was broken and I was the only one left living at home with her. She relied on me a lot as she still couldn't read or write and each day I read the daily paper to her as my Da had always done. Our Albert lived just across the street and all my other brothers were close by. Dickie also did lots for Ma and he and Sally took her everywhere with them. There wasn't a day that passed when Ma didn't cry; her heart was so sore after Da's death.

About a year after Da died I was working on the foundations at Musgrave Park Hospital when my thoughts strayed to Da and how I missed him. I began to cry and the tears were running down my cheeks. Our Sammy saw me. 'Why are you crying wee lad?' he asked. I told him I wasn't crying and that it was only water running down my cheeks. 'You're crying about our Da, aren't you?' he questioned. 'Well, if Da saw you crying now he'd be laughing at you,' he said. I started laughing and after that I felt a whole lot better.

I had just bought my first car from my brother Jim and paid him the princely sum of £25. It was a Riley saloon and was British racing green with a sunroof and a windscreen that opened up. The doors opened from front to rear like all the vintage cars did. It was my pride and joy. I didn't have a driving licence nor had I any insurance for the car, but that didn't seem important to me at the time. All I wanted to do was impress Anne when she came up to the house. We would drive around the Whitewell estate with the windscreen open.

'You didn't tell me you could drive, George,' Anne stated.

'I can do a lot of things that you don't know about,' I answered cleverly.

'When did you pass your test then?' she asked.

'Oh, donkeys ago,' I replied, while getting concerned that she was asking too many questions.

'Why don't you come up to collect me in the car then?'

'Because I've work to do on it,' I lied.

Ma waved her finger sternly at me one day, saying, 'Listen to me young fella, if you take that lovely girl out in that car again without having a driving licence and insurance, I'm going to sell it on you.'

'Ma, don't talk a load of rubbish,' I replied.

'You're going to drive it and knock some poor child down or kill yourself, if you do it once more I will sell it.'

However, I ignored her advice and didn't believe she would carry out her threat.

I arrived home from work one day to discover my beautiful Riley had disappeared from the front door. 'Where's my car, Ma?'

'That's it on the mantle-piece,' she told me, pointing at the fireplace.

'There's only a fiver sitting there Ma,' I protested, 'where's my car?' Ma had sold the car to the Gypsies. I was angry with Ma, but the car was gone and she didn't know where it had been taken. In time I knew that Ma was right and that she only did what was best for me, but it took a long time before I forgave her.

Anne

Chapter Fourteen

Wee Geordie Marries

During the summer of 1966 I received the sum of £1,200 as compensation for my eye injury. England also won the World Cup at Wembley, so it wasn't a bad summer.

Bob Harbinson also gave me his blessing when I asked him if I could marry Anne. He didn't agree straight away, but quizzed me about the future and how I would support and look after her. I told him I was going to build a house when I could afford it and I suppose that may have convinced him. However, I was aware that part of his reluctance was due to the fact that his own marriage had broken down when Anne's mother had left him for a man who was a bricklayer. As far as I was concerned, his fears were totally unfounded. I was going to marry his daughter for life.

A few days later we went to a jeweller in Belfast where one of Anne's sisters worked. I bought Anne an engagement ring, a solitaire diamond, and paid £190 cash for it. We celebrated our engagement after her late shift with our favourite meal of fish and chips.

Things were definitely looking up. I no longer had to catch the bus home after seeing Anne as I had bought my very own Honda 50cc motorcycle with some of the cash from my eye injury. That meant I could spend longer with Anne who had now moved to her own nurse's apartment with its own kitchen. My only problem was, I hadn't planned for rain. On leaving quite late one evening I heard rain on the windows. It was summer time and I had arrived wearing only a suit and had no helmet or coat. The only thing I could do was borrow a coat and headscarf from Anne. Cross-dressing was not my thing and I was thankful I didn't meet anyone else that night!

Anne and I were to be married on 28 July 1967. I was just twenty years old. We planned to buy a new house in Carnmoney from FT Ferguson builders who I'd served my time as a bricklayer with. We chose a beautiful bungalow but almost didn't get it when I discovered that in those days a purchaser had to be at least twenty-one years old. However, I quickly changed my year of birth to 1945! I paid a deposit of £120 and duly signed the contract for our new home. The purchase price was £3,200 and we qualified for a government subsidy of £250 which meant we had a mortgage of £18 each month.

Anne and I were married at her church on 28 July as arranged. Alec was best man and our Sammy was groomsman. I thought the reception afterwards was a grand affair, held at the Abbeylands Hotel in Newtownabbey, but it was the only wedding I'd ever been to when no alcohol was served. Anne's family were all teetotal and therefore drink was definitely not on the menu that day or any other day.

My Ma was a very proud lady. I was her last son to marry and it was the first time for ages Ma had all her sons together in the one place. She had her photograph taken with all of us with her standing in the middle. It was a memorable day in every way.

We went to London for our honeymoon and I flew for the first time on an aeroplane. It didn't all go smoothly. Anne was sick on the plane and when we got to Heathrow Airport I was surprised that it would cost £15 to hire a taxi to take us to the Regent Palace Hotel in Piccadilly where we were to spend the next week.

Imagine my horror when we arrived at the hotel to be told that we had no booking. I insisted they must have a room for us and that I had booked it a long time ago. In addition, it was our honeymoon, so surely they had a room. Luck was on my side when we were eventually offered a room. What I'd failed to tell Anne was that I had completely forgotten to book the hotel! It was years later before I told Anne the truth about this incident.

The hotel cost me £200 for both of us for the week. It was a lot of money in those days. However, we had a wonderful week sightseeing and visiting art galleries. I had booked a final surprise for Anne to round off our honeymoon – dinner in the revolving restaurant of the GPO Tower. I was very excited at the prospect, but only until Anne enquired about our flight times to travel home, then the surprise was all mine. I checked our tickets to discover we had only two hours to get to the airport to catch our flight to Belfast. I was very disappointed about missing the meal I had planned, but fortunately Anne saw the funny side and we both had a good laugh.

Chapter Fifteen

The Family Man

Our new bungalow was ready for us to move into in the September of that year. Money was tight but we were both working. Two months after our wedding we discovered that Anne was pregnant with our first child. We were overjoyed, as were both our families. This was to be the first grandchild in the Harbinson family.

Our son, George Robert, was born in June 1968. Anne gave up nursing and became a full-time mother. We were delighted with our new baby boy who became a very lively and boisterous child. When he was a baby he awoke every two hours for food, we just couldn't fill him. Ma soon taught Anne and I how to keep the child's belly full. She was sitting for us one evening we had gone to see the film *Madame X* starring Lana Turner. On our return the wee man was sleeping heavily; Ma had stuffed him full of stew, you could almost see the meat and carrots through his extended belly but it certainly did the trick. No more sleepless nights, for a short while anyway, but the terry nappies were quite another story!

As he grew Anne couldn't keep up with him, he led her a dance. Always climbing walls and fences and getting into scrapes. He disappeared one day and Anne was frantic. He was found two hours later. I returned home from work and all the neighbourhood was out searching and panic had started to set in. I heard a distinctive rustling sound coming from the direction of our coalbunker and sure enough, as I gazed through the coal shoot, barely visible was the wee man, face and teeth blackened as he had sat there eating on the lumps of coal.

It wasn't long after the birth of George that Anne became pregnant again and our second son, Keith Ross, was born in June 1969. The Americans had just landed on the moon, 'one giant step for mankind' and another big leap for Wee Geordie. Keith was a quieter child; he was no trouble whatsoever. He wasn't as adventurous as his older brother and needed the reassurance of Anne and I. This was probably due to him being hospitalised when he was about a year and a half old.

Both boys from an early age accompanied me on my shooting days when we all tramped over fields and bogs in pursuit of pigeons, snipe and hares. I spent more time trying to find their welly boots which got stuck in the mud than flushing out any snipe or hare. However, they became very efficient at the country pursuits including fishing. I taught them how to clean the game and how to make game pies and stews. They learnt how to gut and clean fish, which came in very useful when both boys were employed at Billy Evans' Wet Fish Shop on Saturdays.

Anne decided that contraception was needed, but too late! In August 1970 Ruth Elizabeth Douglas came into the world. Our family was complete and I realised what a lucky fella I was with a wife and three healthy children. What more could I want?

My other passion in life, beside my family, was my love of paintings. One day, waiting patiently for Anne to finish her shift, I walked into the Belfast library. I had never been in a library before let alone ever read a book. My attention was drawn to a bright yellow book that was out of line from all the rest of the books on the shelf. I looked at it and discovered it was the life story of the Dutch painter Vincent Van Gogh. The book was called *The Man Who Loved the Sun*. I was hooked and joined the library there and then. Now I was a reader of art – not bad for a wee lad from the back streets of Belfast. My love for paintings grew and even though money was scarce I attended every exhibition I could get to and at one event had the great pleasure of meeting Sir Russell Flint who was exhibiting at The Magee Gallery in Belfast. His painting of his favourite model 'Cecilia', who he portrayed topless in various poses, was a stunning painting. What excuses could I make to Anne, the Secretary of the Nurses Christian Fellowship, that a semi-nude painting hanging over the fireplace was much better to look at than a luxury wool carpet? After several cups of strong coffee that day, the luxury green carpet won. Now, the same carpet is threadbare and worthless and 'Cecilia' is still beautiful and worth about £50,000. I often reflect on that decision and vowed never to make the same mistake again.

Chapter Sixteen

Start of the Troubles

In 1969 the 'Troubles' in Northern Ireland had started with civil rights marches in Belfast and Londonderry. I was back working with my brothers and Jackie, who had all returned from America. We were employed building bathrooms for the terraced houses in the White Rock Road. This was a predominantly Roman Catholic area, but it didn't matter to us. The people living in the area knew who we were and that we originated from the Protestant Shankill Road. We never had any problems; in fact, they were more than good to us. Some days it became difficult to decide which house to go to for lunch as we had so many invitations. The people were all so kind. They knew we were members of the Orange Order. One elderly lady who had been watching the twelfth of July parades said to us, 'Bless you boys. I saw you on the telly. I bet your Ma and Da are proud of all of you's. You all looked so smart.' Unfortunately, things were to change over the summer and were never to be the same again.

The Orange Order Association was formed in England in 1688 to advance the interest of William, 3rd Prince of

Orange, and who on 1st July,1690, defeated the combined forces of popery and tyranny in Ireland after the Battle of the Diamond in 1795. The Order was reorganized and formed into lodges for the defence of Protestantism and for the mutual defence and support of Irish Protestants.

Civil Rights marches took place and both sides of the sectarian divide took revenge against each other. Religious beliefs have haunted the Irish Nation for over 300 years.

It was Friday 15 August 1969 and my brothers, Jackie and I drove to work at Whiterock Gardens. Things seemed different that day, very quiet and you could have cut the atmosphere with a knife. People were going about their business, but no one seemed to talk very much and others stayed indoors. I hadn't seen the local news but a lady in the street told me the 'B' Specials had shot dead a Catholic man who had done nothing but was just walking home. 'Why would they do that?' I asked her. I couldn't understand what was going on.

'Because he was a Catholic, that's all,' she replied. The 'B' Specials were a Police Reserve Force that supported the regular Royal Ulster Constabulary. They were formed in the 1920s to counteract the Irish Republican Army (IRA) activities throughout previous years in Northern Ireland. I could not understand the hostility, as we had always been happy working and living amongst decent people. We were well liked when building in the area and I had a good rapport with the wee bucks. I played football with them at lunch times and when they finished school they would carry bricks for me in return for a little pocket money.

Liam O'Donnell, a friend of our Albert's visited him on that Friday. He had a haulage business in the Whiterock Gardens. He advised Albert to get us off the job as there was going to be trouble. He was certainly in the know as he was a member of the official IRA, but a decent and hard-working man. Albert told Jackie and me to leave our tools and go and he crossed the road to tell Alec and Sammy.

'What are you doing Jackie?' I asked.

'Packing up and getting off this job,' he replied, shouting up the scaffolding to me.

'Well, I'm not fucking going off any job. There's no one forcing me to go anywhere. I have a wife and children to feed and a mortgage to pay.'

'Geordie, you'll have to pack up,' Jackie insisted. I ignored him. I had only just made another pile of mortar and I wasn't going anywhere. Jackie went off to speak to Alec and Sammy.

'Hey you. Who the fuck do you think you are?'

I turned around when I heard the gruff Derry accent.

'What the fuck has it got to do with you?' I scoffed at the young rough-looking fella who was shouting up to me.

'If you don't get off this fucking job you'll be carried off in a box. You might be a friend of Liam O'Donnell's but you're no friend of mine,' he added.

'Why are you going to do it then, do you think you can put me off this job?' I argued sarcastically.

He lifted his jacket so I could see the handle of the revolver he had shoved down his belt. 'This will put you off then,' he said.

I stood looking down at him from the scaffold with my trowel in my hand. 'Would you be as brave without the gun?' I shouted.

'I'm gonna give you five minutes to get off this site, and if you don't you'll be going out in a box.'

He walked away. Luckily for me my brothers arrived and demanded I join them on the ground. We're leaving. I was angry when we left our tools behind and so could not work.

Trouble broke out all over Northern Ireland. Catholics and Protestants burnt each other out of their houses. My Da's brother, Uncle Frank, and his wife, Aunt Mary Anne, telephoned me and asked for help to get them out of their house in Ballynure Street, off the Oldpark Road. Throngs of people were coming from over The Bone, a Catholic area, and forcing Protestants out of their homes. I hired a van and with our Sammy and went to Uncle Frank's. We loaded up the van with all his furniture. Aunt Mary Anne was crying uncontrollable. I was so angry that people couldn't live in peace with one another.

An aggressive crowd had gathered in the street while we were loading up the van. They constantly chanted and jeered and one man even had the cheek to ask to look round the house. 'What for?' I asked sharply. I was in no mood for pleasantries.

'I'm taking over this house,' he replied cheekily.

'That's what you fucking think, but it will be over my dead body,' I bawled at him.

'If that's what you want then that won't be a problem,' he said. Sammy heard the commotion and grabbed me and pulled me indoors.

'Fuck-em Sammy, they're not getting this house.' I was so outraged I took a hammer and proceeded to smash the wash-hand basin and toilet. I then turned all the gas on with the intent of burning the whole place to the ground. If my aunt and uncle couldn't live there then no one else would. Sammy again grabbed me and dragged me into the street.

We were lucky to get away when we did as the crowd were becoming more angry and hostile.

My Uncle Frank and Aunt Mary Anne had owned their home in Ballynure Street and I was angry that it had been taken from them without a penny and that they were forced to squat in a Housing Executive house.

The British Army had arrived on the streets of Northern Ireland and the rioting was out of control. Initially they were welcomed with open arms by the Catholic community, but this welcome was short lived and they were soon to be turned on ferociously.

Work was difficult to find and I'd no money coming in. I was sick of being controlled by these bastards and I asked Albert what he was doing about our work commitments. He told me the Army had blocked the roads to the Whiterock area and that the IRA were shooting at the Army. It wasn't a good place to go to work.

I wasn't having any of it. 'Fuck the IRA and the Army'. I intended to get our tools back and start back to work as soon as possible.

Without Albert knowing, I instructed his lorry driver to take me to the Whiterock area. We set off but the driver refused to go any further when he saw the barricades at the end of the road. 'You're fucking nuts, you'll get yourself shot,' he told me, and he was probably right. I told him to get out and wait for me and started to drive up the road.

'Halt!' a soldier shouted pointing a rifle at me as I approached the barrier.

'I work up here and I intend going through that barrier to get my tools,' I shouted to him. He repeated that I couldn't go any further.

'This is the fucking Queen's highway and I'm going up to get my tools.'

With this another soldier interrupted and ordered, 'Let him through. If he wants to get his lorry burned, fuck him.'

I drove the lorry through the barrier until I saw Father Murphy who knew me. 'You shouldn't be up here Geordie, it's too dangerous and I can't guarantee your safety.'

'Father, we've no money and we need to get back to work up here,' I told him. Father Murphy accompanied me up through the barricades of burnt-out cars and vans. It looked like a war zone. After speaking to some of the people Father Murphy said that they would be glad to see us back working so that we could finish building the bathrooms but that he could not guarantee our safety.

Our Albert was mad at me, but nevertheless we did manage to finish the job, even though we had to drive behind the barricades every day and the risks were great.

Chapter Seventeen

Big Decisions

In 1970 the Troubles throughout the country got so bad there was very little work. I'd been earning a good wage as a bricklayer but now money was scarce and I knew our savings wouldn't last forever. Drastic measures had to be taken, so together with Alex, Sammy and Jackie I went to work in England at Strike Command Headquarters in High Wycombe, Buckinghamshire. We were working a week in advance prior to payment, but the money was poor and the money I sent Anne didn't cover the bills. After this job we went to work in Aberystwyth in Wales building the halls of residence at the university there. We had been away for about five or six weeks when Anne became desperate for money and wrote to me asking for cash to pay bills and buy food. She had even used up the coins we had saved in a plastic bag in the wardrobe that had amounted to about seven pounds.

We were shortly to return home when a job turned up at Musgrave Park Hospital, building a new extension to the orthopaedic department. The money wasn't any better but at least we were all with our families.

Work was still scarce and the troubles between Republicans and Loyalists continued to divide the community. My brothers and I were all members of the Orange Order and attended meetings at the local Orange Hall.

I attended a meeting at our local Orange Hall to discuss security in our area. Policemen were under attack in their own homes by Republicans. It was decided that each local man would have the responsibility of helping the police by walking and driving around at night to observe strangers and strange vehicles in the area. I was in agreement with this practice. But I was not in agreement with earlier talk of people arming themselves with illegal firearms and explosives, which could apparently be acquired from the continent. I realised things were becoming out of control. People were genuinely concerned they were losing the battle against the IRA and were preparing to take the law into their own hands in order to protect themselves. I was not prepared to go down this road.

After long discussions with both Anne and my brothers, we decided that our best interests lay with the forces of law and order. I told Anne I was not prepared to go along with anything illegal as had been suggested at the recent meeting. She supported me, although she was very cautious and asked me whether it was worth me risking my life for fifty pence an hour. That's all the police reservists were paid in those early days. However, we all joined the part-time police reservists. We were brickies by day and police reservists by night in our spare time. We were trained in the use of firearms for our own protection, and use if necessary. We were stationed in Newtownabbey. Sammy and I patrolled together and each carried a .38 Webley revolver with five rounds of ammunition for protection. How anyone thought five rounds would ever protect us if we were attacked by the IRA, who would be armed to the teeth, I'll never know.

We thought we looked smart and were proud of our new Royal Ulster Constabulary uniforms with American flak jackets. The flak jackets were previously worn by American soldiers and some still had the original names on them. It was cold at night as we walked around the dark streets. I always wore old pyjama bottoms underneath my trousers when it was very cold; they also stopped the trousers rubbing on the top of my legs, which could be quite painful when I had to do a lot of walking.

When I looked through the windows as we passed along the streets I saw families looking cosy and warm sitting in front of the fire. How I longed to be at home with my family, but I knew that the job had to be done in order for communities to be safe.

On our first night on duty, Sammy and I were called to the home of a lady who had her windows broken at the back of her house, presumably attempted burglary. We filled in three pages of our notebook and measured up for glass and putty telling her we would be back the following day to replace the broken windows. The Sergeant laughed when we returned to the station and reported on our 'repair service'. He commended us on a thorough job but warned us not to carry out the repair service on a regular basis as everyone would expect the same treatment which not all police officers would be able to provide!

In contrast, the next night we were sitting in bushes armed with a Stirling sub-machine gun watching for an IRA gang who had blown up a bookmaker's home and murdered him. It was expected the gang would return and Sammy and I were instructed to lie in wait. It was a very tense time as the slightest movement could have blown our cover. The bookmaker's cat nearly got shot when it emerged from the bushes near where I was lying. Lucky cat, I thought, as the hairs on the back of my neck bristled.

It wasn't just the IRA we were dealing with. The other side of the sectarian divide was the Loyalist Para-militaries. They didn't like the police much either and because they didn't feel that the police protected them enough they often took the law into their own hands. The Ulster Defence Association started carrying out sectarian murders and targeting Catholics.

An innocent Catholic man from the Doagh Road had been working on his car. He was gunned down on his own doorstop – shot in the back by some coward. His wife and five children were weeping over his body when I arrived at the scene. I vowed there and then that if ever anyone hurt a member of my family they wouldn't begin to know what a terrorist was. I later learned that it was the so-called Paramilitaries who had brutally murdered this man just because of his religion.

Every night the violence continued resulting in the killing of innocent people. One night while working near my own home we called in with Anne for tea, sandwiches and homemade buns. Before leaving I called Glengormley police station to be told that one of our colleagues had been shot while on routine patrol duty. A sniper had hit Jack Rogers as he stood outside The Glen Inn public house. He too was a part-time police officer in his late forties and was married with two children. He was a decent man, a good colleague and all he ever wanted to do was stop people murdering each other. I felt sad and angry that a man like Jack had been gunned down so brutally simply because he was a member of the police force.

Chapter Eighteen

Decision Made

'Why don't you stay in tonight George? You've worked hard all week and you look tired,' Anne said. I wasn't spending much time at home these days and I was seeing very little of Anne and the kids, but I had to do what I thought was right.

'They are short of a man Anne, and we have to be down there at 7.00pm tonight,' I answered. So much was happening in the community that every man was needed. Anne was worried and told me she prayed for me all the time I was out. I drove to the station that evening in my white Mini 1000 wearing part uniform. It would have been too dangerous to travel in full uniform.

Parading for duty the sergeant said, 'George, I want you and Mary Ray to go in your car and patrol the area. We are expecting an attack; be vigilant and report any incidents.' Over the radio we heard that a car had been abandoned on the O'Neill Road near the junction of the Doagh Road. Its lights were on and the doors open and the engine was still running. This transmission was to another unit but we still made our way to lend support. We saw the Land Rover, Delta 19, drive into O'Neill

Road and followed close behind. Shooting began immediately from the high ground on the nearside of our vehicle. The target was the police Land Rover. I saw the muzzle flashes from the guns and heard each round strike the Land Rover.

'Get down, get down,' I heard as I got out of my vehicle. I fell to my knees and saw a uniformed officer fall out of the back of the Land Rover. 'I've been hit!' he shouted. 'My back,' he said as he collapsed in the road. I ran over and lifted him in my arms. I carried him over to my Mini and placed him in the back seat. Whiteabbey Hospital was only 500 yards away and I sped to the door. I lifted my colleague in my arms and kicked the doors. A nurse shouted that the door was not in use and that we had to go to the front door.

'This man's been shot, get a fucking doctor!' I yelled. Having gained access, I placed my colleague on a trolley and removed his boots and trousers. His leg was bleeding badly. I never knew who the officer was but I do know that he survived. I sustained nothing more than a back injury, which kept me off work for two weeks, and fortunately I had my personal nurse at home.

These experiences made me realise that I wanted to join the regular police force. I wanted to be able to spend more time helping to prevent mayhem, murder and maiming of my fellow police officers, and do more to protect the decent people of Northern Ireland. I applied to join the police full time and took a considerable drop in pay although I believed the job would be a lot more secure with future prospects. I also felt I would attain a certain degree of respectability, as by now I was living amongst business people who were white-collar workers.

I was later to find out it was a costly career change, in more ways than one.

Thankfully my children were healthy and happy. Anne didn't want me to give up building. I suppose she worried about my safety although she didn't say a lot and always supported my decisions.

Chapter Nineteen

The New Family House

I'd seen a nice plot of land in a place called Templepatrick. The house I'd promised to build for Anne was now going to be a reality. I could buy the plot for £4000 and, against Anne's wishes I borrowed money from the bank to buy it. My family was again growing and we were blessed with another daughter who we named Sarah Jane.

Building the bungalow commenced in October 1975 with the help of Sammy, Jackie and a hodsman from the Falls Road – a Catholic friend. I had calculated for every penny spent; the cost of the timber, bricks, even the mortar. I was so proud that I was eventually fulfilling my dream and proving to the doubters in Anne's family.

I'd ordered special coloured mortar to match the sandstone bricks and things were looking good. The last brick was put in place and I informed the joiner the peaks had been built and the building was now ready for the roof to go on.

The timber had arrived and I'd erected all the scaffolding ready for the joiner to commence. He promised he'd be with me the next day but failed to appear on site. I was worried because the weather forecast was not good and we were expecting high winds and storms. I didn't sleep that night and at 7am I was up and out to check on the building and the new peaks. Happily, they were still in situ, so feeling more contented I returned home for breakfast. The wind was still blowing a gale. I returned to the site shortly afterwards and to my dismay saw one of the peaks had collapsed inwards, crashing through the scaffolding, smashing planks and trestles.

I was utterly dismayed. There was no more money for new bricks or mortar; what was I going to do? The rain was coming down in buckets; I sat myself on a pile of the bricks and with a bricklaying scotch I started to clean every brick as the rain poured down the back of my neck and the tears poured down my cheeks. I knew if I didn't do it there and then I would never have finished my bungalow. It took me the whole of that cold wet January day to clean off the bricks, eventually giving up at 7pm because I could no longer see what I was doing.

I devoured the joiner on the telephone when I spoke to him. 'You promised me faithfully you'd be there to put the roof on,' I bellowed at him. 'You call yourself a Christian? Some fucking Christian you are.'

I had to buy new yellow mortar but saved the bricks. He said how sorry he was and attended the next day to put the roof on. The ironic thing was he also tried to buy the bungalow from me.

I eventually finished the bungalow and we moved in on a beautiful summer day in May 1976. I continued bricklaying until such time that my application was being processed for the police. I was looking forward to wearing the uniform and I felt it would give me a sort of status.

Returning home from building one day I was unnerved to see my sons George and Keith riding around a neighbour's garden in their toy tractor and trailer, delivering small deposits of sand and strategically placing them all over the driveway and lawns. I gave off to Anne for not keeping her eyes on the boys, and was just about to leave the house to sweep up the deposits when the neighbour jumped across my garden wall in a fit of temper, ranting and raving at me about the mess in his garden. I had the brush and shovel in my hand and told him I'd just arrived home and was about to clear it up. 'You'd better get it cleared up, and I'll tell you something else, you'd better keep those wee bastards out of my garden or I'll stick my toe up their arses.'

'Hold on a minute Mister, one thing my children aren't, they're not bastards, and if you lift your hands to my children I'll flatten you.' I was starting to get annoyed at his attitude but was trying to keep calm, as the children were present.

'Oh will you indeed? In that case why don't you come on and see what you can do?' he challenged. I put the brush and shovel down and we went out to the grassy verge.

'You'd better take your jacket off,' I suggested. 'I'll not need my own jacket off to beat the likes of you.'

Bloody hell, I thought, I'm going to get a hiding here. This is what it must have been like for my Da and

Uncle Jim when they were bare-fist fighting in the Chapel Fields. But I was not doing it for money; I was doing it for my family. His offer to fight was to his demise; he made a wild lunge at me to which I responded with a straight left, followed by a right hook. That was it; the fight was over. I'd knocked him to the ground. There he was holding his head and bleeding from his eye and nose.

A few people had gathered round to watch the melee when one wee woman shouted, 'Aye, you've met your match now, you'll not threaten anyone else in the street the way you threatened my wee Tommy. You've done a good job Geordie; he's threatened everyone in the street at some time or another; he deserves all he gets.'

I made my way back to the house; sadly, George and Keith had seen me fighting with the man. I collected the brush and shovel and cleaned up the sand from the man's garden. I knocked at his door and was going to apologise to him. I sincerely regretted my hasty actions.

'That was a big mistake,' his wife told me as I stood on their doorstep. 'He certainly met his match this time. He's in the bath being sick, please go through.' I was surprised she invited me in or even spoke to me as she had watched the whole event and at one point she was swinging around my neck trying to stop me from hitting him again.

'Look Mister, I'm sorry for what happened but you threatened to hit my children.'

'You're right, Mr Douglas, I deserved all I got,' he said sheepishly. I couldn't believe he reacted the way he did; he took it all in good spirit and turned out to be a decent enough fella after all.

I did panic a bit as my application was still going through to join the police. I was lucky he didn't report me and I was grateful to him for that. I was fiercely protective of my family and tended to take the law into my own hands. You know the saying, 'If you want something done then do it yourself'; at least you feel the satisfaction. My fear expressed itself in anger, it was the only way I knew how in those days.

I was normally a quiet man and Anne and I kept ourselves very much to ourselves. It was only when Anne complained to me one day that the young couple with no children who had moved in down the road were driving their red MG sports car furiously up and down the street, that I too saw red. I stepped out in front of the car the next opportunity I had. The driver, a young man, slammed on his brakes and skidded to a halt, inches in front of me. 'Are you fucking stupid? I nearly knocked you down,' he bellowed at me.

'No, I'm not fucking stupid, you are, driving at speeds like that in a street full of children. You've no children now but one day you will have. I have two children and if you knock them down I will fucking kill you, do you understand me. Don't be driving this car up and down this street like a mad man or I'll stuff it up your fucking arse.'

I think he understood me, judging by the astonished look on his face! A few hours later he came to our door to apologise, 'You're right Mr Douglas, I have certainly been driving too fast,' he told me and again I apologised for my outburst. After this altercation he always drove slowly down the street and used to gesture a friendly neighbourly wave to me in passing. I suppose he appreciated how I felt when he eventually had children of his own.

My garden was now looking lovely, and so it should have. I followed the instructions precisely from the book *The Perfect Lawn*. Having marked the garden with lengths of string in square yards, I carefully weighed the grass seed on Anne's weighing scales – 2 ounces per square yard. The lawn looked spectacular and all my neighbours congratulated me on my beautiful lawn. It was emerald green, cut to perfection with long straight lines. It was my boyhood dream to have a beautiful lawn. 'One day I'm gonna have a beautiful lawn like that Jimmy,' I said to my childhood friend Jimmy Neil. We were about nine years old then and were standing gazing at the most cracking garden the two of us had ever seen. We were in the Antrim Road, near to Belfast Castle where we were going for the day.

As we marvelled and dreamed at the site before our longing eyes, the man whose garden it was, walked down to us and without any prior warning lashed a bucket of water over us. 'Clear off you wee shits; I know what you's are up to.' We weren't up to anything, the shock mesmerised us both, and we were only looking at the man's nice garden and had no malice in our thoughts, only admiration. We didn't have a garden at our homes, just orange boxes and old baths and sinks filled with Sweet William and Orange Lilies, ready for the twelfth of July.

'Fuck you, you old bastard,' I yelled out, 'we were only looking at your nice garden.' He pretended to run after us but we scarpered, wet through.

Ironically, thirty years later a man and lady from the same area in Antrim Road came to buy the first bungalow I'd built in Templepatrick and commented on my lovely lawn!

Chapter Twenty

The New Recruit

My application to join the full time police service was successful and I went to the police-training centre in Enniskillen for fourteen weeks in August of that year.

I found my time at the training centre difficult. I had worked for myself for so long that I found it difficult to accept orders from others. I also struggled with the academic aspects of training. However, it all came good in the end when I was placed twenty-seventh out of ninety-six recruits in the final examinations. Not bad, I thought, for a boy who was educated at a 'special' school.

My first posting as a full-time uniformed officer was to York Road police station. This station was located on a road that ran parallel to Belfast Lough on the North side. It was a working-class part of Belfast that took in the notorious Tiger Bay area that was staunchly protestant and UDA territory. The outlawed Ulster Freedom Fighters (UFF) and Ulster Volunteer Force (UVF) were regularly active within this area. On occasions we would cover the New Lodge Road district that was mainly Catholic and was totally controlled by the IRA.

We were equipped with a personal firearm. Mine was a Walther 9 millimetre semi-automatic pistol. On board vehicles there would be either a Stirling 9 millimetre sub-machine gun or an Ml Carbine – not for the faint-hearted.

All Land Rovers and other police vehicles were armoured. The doors were heavy and awkward to manoeuvre. Some officers had difficulty getting in and out of them, especially the less fit. The body armour didn't help our mobility either, as it was heavy and I often wondered what would have happened if I'd fallen on my back; how would I get up? It had a hard shell, front and back, with straps over each shoulder and on the sides to secure it in place.

Some officers suffered back injuries with the weight of the body armour, but it was compulsory to wear. In time we were supplied with new flexible flak jackets, and although they were still heavy, they were much more comfortable to move about in.

The experience gained when I was in the reserve force stood me in good stead and I was now prepared for a more active part in the fight against terrorism. I was happy enough in my work but I still found it difficult to take orders from others, who although senior in rank to me, I believed were less experienced in life than I was.

I was involved in a variety of routine work, simple thefts and routine enquiries and incidents. However, routine duties in Northern Ireland were completely different to normal policing elsewhere. The IRA consistently targeted us and we could never drop our guard for fear of being shot at.

David Purse was a young part-time policeman and was on routine police duty directing traffic. He was detailed to direct traffic outside the Crusaders Football ground on the Shore Road one Saturday afternoon. An IRA unit who were from the New Lodge Road district fatally gunned him down. On the previous Saturday I was the policeman directing the traffic at the Crusaders ground. It wasn't my time!

I had dealt with a number of cases of theft and other serious crimes which necessitated me working closely with my detective colleagues from the Criminal Investigation Department and around this time I was approached by the detective inspector of one station who suggested I should apply for the Criminal Investigation Department. To many a young officer the CID Interview Board was daunting, but one had to pass this difficult interview, presided over by three senior officers in order to become a detective, which so many young officers dreamed of and worked hard for. I had prepared seriously for this interview and hoped the questions would fall in my favour.

I entered the room at Garnerville Training Centre full of confidence. I was greeted by three high-ranking officers who were sitting behind a large desk and looking very formal. I was ready for any questions they threw at me.

'Come in Constable Douglas and have a seat,' they instructed. I was previously told how to sit in the chair, with my hands clasped and resting on top of my knees.

I spoke clearly and explained to them the qualities I believed I had in order to be a successful detective officer. I knew by this time in my career it was the route I wished to take.

They questioned me on my reasons for wanting to become a detective officer, and I reciprocated by speaking clearly. They bombarded me with question after question, most of which I managed to answer. On the whole the interview seemed to be going well.

'What do you know about identification parades then, Constable Douglas?' I couldn't believe they had just asked that question as I had just finished my two days per month probationary training, and the last subject we had covered was all about identification parades.

'Quite a bit,' I answered foolishly.

'Oh, really? Let's see how much you know then,' one of the panel said. I thought I answered each question well. 'You do know quite a lot about identification parades, you must have studied this area well,' the same officer added. I agreed with him and again felt happy with how things were going, but just as I thought I'd cracked it, the crippler came!

'Constable Douglas, what would you do if your suspect had a club foot?' My confidence suddenly diminished as I pondered the question – what would I do?

'That's one question I'm going to have to think about,' I told the panel.

'So you really don't know everything about identification parades, isn't that right?' the chairman said. I had to agree.

'Yes, Sir, you're right, I don't; but I will find the answer.' With my tail between my legs I made my way to the door. I turned to look back and all three officers were smiling at each other. At that moment I had a stroke of genius.

'I've got it Sir,' I said, 'I'd ask them to sit down and put their legs underneath them.' They all simultaneously burst out laughing.

'Thank you very much Detective Constable Douglas,' the chairman said.

I punched the air outside the door. 'Yes, I've done it!' I shouted. Little did I know that the half-hour interview was to change my life completely.

Chapter Twenty-One

Detective Douglas, 'Big Geordie'

My first posting as a detective was to Castlereagh CID office. Investigation became a paramount part of my work and it wasn't long before I was thrown in at the deep end. My respect for my fellow detectives was high. These were men and women who had lots of experience and I valued their integrity.

I was sent to a murder scene on the Mill Vale Road in Bessbrook together with two other detectives. One of the officers was on secondment from the Lancashire Constabulary. I drove the armoured vehicle to the army camp at Bessbrook. This was routine in order that the army could provide escort to the scene of crime. We were going to a very Republican area that we called 'Bandit Country', South Armagh.

The carnage that met us there was sickening. There was little left of the RUC Land Rover. Five officers had been returning to their base at Bessbrook when a white van, packed with IRA explosives, was detonated by remote control just as the Land Rover was passing by. The vehicle and the men were completely blown to pieces. I was revolted at what I saw and I felt hatred towards the bastards who did this in the so-called name of Ireland. This was blind hatred of men in uniforms, trying to do a job for their country. My heart cried for these men, their wives, parents and children. However, we had to continue to function. We had to try to investigate this case and assist in bringing the perpetrators to justice.

The investigation was difficult in itself, but in South Armagh, where members of the Crown Forces were hated, we had to be accompanied at all times by the army and uniformed colleagues. Front doors were slammed in our faces and abuse thrown at us from every household when we were required to make house-to-house enquiries. When I was withdrawn from this murder enquiry, which was to be progressed by local detectives, I returned to Castlereagh station with hatred in my heart.

I continued to be involved on a day-to-day basis investigating violent incidents, murders, shootings and bombings. It was relentless. I would go home and lie in bed questioning my own ability to do this job. I knew I was becoming hardened and more determined to bring these murderers to justice. I wasn't prepared to let anything or anybody stand in my way. I called it 'Big Geordie Law'. I played by my rules!

The IRA and UVF didn't like my rules, even though it was their rules I was playing by. If they wanted to play this game, then I'm their man.

Castlereagh was the holding centre for all terrorist suspects. Behind high metal railings was a ramshackle of old porta-cabins. Part of the old building had been damaged by a bomb explosion a number of years earlier and consequently was replaced by temporary buildings. They were most uncomfortable, hot in summer and cold in winter, not the best of conditions even for us 'peelers'.

On the ground floor of the buildings there were cells, where all terrorist prisoners were housed. Each cell had painted walls and an iron bed with a mattress and a chair that was chained to the bed. Although the cells were clean they were stark and crude with no windows and therefore no natural light.

Prisoners had the use of showers that were at the end of each unit and they were supplied with toiletries. However, the smell of the whole environment remains with me to this day. It is the smell of fear that exudes from the human body when it is under pressure. I always had to shower immediately after leaving work to remove the stench from my body, nostrils and clothes.

Prisoners were defiant of any authority. Some felt they were above the law and even refused to conform to requests to leave their cells to be interviewed. Defecation and urination was commonplace by these anti-authoritarians. Such a code of behaviour was apparently their anti-interrogation tactics which were taught to them. They had been taught these measures by the IRA anti-interrogation courses, which their members were compelled to attend.

After the murders of two of my uniformed colleagues, who were tragically gunned down in Belfast City Centre by a close quarter assassination gun team, a number of IRA suspects were arrested. The two officers were brutally murdered on a Saturday morning when women and children shopped in the city centre streets. Few people came forward with any positive evidence, although witnesses did come forward and gave false information. It was a difficult task.

One of these suspects I was detailed to interview was a notorious leader of the Irish National Liberation Army (INLA). This was a breakaway organisation from the mainstream republican IRA. They were also murderers and hardened terrorists. I had not personally interviewed this man before but his reputation preceded him. He hadn't as yet met 'Big Geordie', but I wanted to meet him. I opened up the cell door. He was lying stripped totally naked on the iron bed – another anti-interrogation tactic. Greeting me in the entrance to the cell was a pile of human faeces.

'What delicacy might this be, Mr O'Kane?' I enquired. He stared at me, still lying on his bed. His hand went to his penis and he began to masturbate, trying to intimidate and indicating that it was me who was the 'wanker.' 'It's time for your interview, Mr O'Kane,' I said. My feelings inside were utter revulsion, but I would never let him see this.

'You can do this interview in two ways,' I explained. 'You can put on your clothes and clear up your own shit, or I can help you to put on your clothes and clean up the shit, if you like.' He ignored both options and continued to masturbate.

'Is this yours?' I asked, as I held the shit in my hand. 'You will need to bring this with you, Mr O'Kane; we can't expect others to clean up after you.' He continued in his defiant manner as his shit was held over his face. It slid through my fingers onto his body and, as the saying goes, that's when the shit hit the fan. As he struggled to get up off the bed, it went everywhere – up his nose and into his mouth. The stench was vile and we were both covered in it.

The guards arrived and restrained O'Kane and ablutions were administered. I had to shower and change before returning to a clean cell where O'Kane was fully clothed, smelling fresher and awaiting my interview with him.

He calmly accompanied me to the interview room BF13, a windowless room around seven feet square with a desk and three plastic chairs, and of course a cigarette bin.

Prisoners' rights were read and questioning commenced. O'Kane was known never to speak when at Castlereagh. This was also part of the anti-interrogation tactics taught by the IRA. However, on this occasion he did speak, but only to deny any involvement with the murders of the two policemen in the city centre and to make a complaint against me. He suggested I'd threatened him that his murdering days were over and that he and his henchmen would be dead by Christmas.

By sheer luck and coincidence, O'Kane was shot dead in his home by two masked gunmen. They shot him fourteen times to make sure his life of murder was well and truly over. In my opinion he was of no loss to society. What goes around comes around.

It was well known when terrorists were interviewed and then released from Castlereagh that on their release each and every one of them was re-interviewed by the

IRA security team. We were beginning to be very successful in recruiting informants from both Republican and Loyalist, as their anti-interrogation courses were failing them. Great inroads were being made by the efforts of detectives in the Crime Squad at Castlereagh. We were successful in finding hide after hide of terrorist weapons and it was becoming increasingly more difficult for the terrorists to operate. Whenever there were large arrests of Republican terrorists, their commanding officers in the IRA ran off South to the Irish Republic, where they could move more freely with impunity.

The border areas between the two countries were farmed by many Protestant farmers. Many of them along the counties of Fermanagh, Tyrone and Armagh borders had their lives taken from them by ethnic cleansing by the IRA's murder gangs. These vulnerable Ulster Protestant farmers, whose only crime was trying to earn an honest living and who harmed no-one.

Although Protestant terrorists were equally as vicious as the Republicans they were not in the same league when it came to being devious and cunning. There was no hardship for us detectives when these people were interviewed. No sooner were they in Castlereagh when they started admitting their crimes, and some were willing to turn informant.

The Loyalists, at that time, didn't have the organisational ability nor the financial support that the IRA were getting from people such as the 'Irish Americans'. The Loyalists funded themselves by committing robberies and racketeering exploits within Northern Ireland against their own people. Because of the IRA campaign in the border areas against the farmers, the Loyalists felt it was necessary and their right to retaliate against any person who was of the Catholic faith. Any Catholic was a legitimate target in their eyes. The belief by then was that the IRA was supported by all Catholics and particularly the Catholic Church. They couldn't understand why the Catholic Church would not excommunicate IRA men who committed murder and were happy to perform the last rites on them, but yet more willing to excommunicate a Catholic priest because he exercised his Christian belief to re-marry Catholics within his church, who had previously divorced.

Martin Finn was a Catholic who was friends with a Loyalist gang of thugs. This ill-founded friendship was to cost Finn his life. The gang that included Finn carried out robberies and burglaries in the Belfast area. As a result of a number of murders against the Ulster Defence Regiment members (part and full-time members of the British Army) along the Fermanagh/Tyrone borders, the gang decided to take revenge on a Catholic person, any Catholic would do, and Martin Finn was the unfortunate chosen person.

They all met in a bar in East Belfast, a loyalist area of the city, on the pretence of committing a robbery. Martin Finn was also present, but unknown to him a murderous plan had been hatched. A member of the gang, Gerard Malone, was to tell me, after many hours of interview, the full details of how Finn was brutally murdered. I received information from a colleague that Malone may be helpful in identifying a man whose nickname was 'Sevenstone' who was allegedly involved in this murder.

I spent a long time interviewing Malone, who sat opposite me with the desk between us. He was a thin boy in his late twenties with dirty fair hair. He hadn't said very much, only to deny his involvement.

'Do you know anyone by the name of Sevenstone?' I enquired. This question seemed to have a debilitating effect on Malone, as I watched him closely. His eyes were transfixed on mine and he had beads of sweat trickling down his forehead. I continued to engage this line of enquiry. I knew he was hiding something and I continued to persist. He held out for a long time, quite a few hours, but eventually began to give me the information I required.

'I'm Sevenstone, Geordie,' he told me. Those were the first words he had spoken since I had originally asked the question.

'Did you kill Michael Finn?' I questioned.

'No, I just drove the car,' he replied. He then told me how he and the gang had met in a pub in East Belfast and had pretended, in front of Finn, to plan a robbery.

Malone drove the gang to a garage in East Belfast. They all got out of the vehicle and walked into the garage. One of the gang pulled out a gun and shot Finn in the head. They continued to batter him over his head with a hammer until he was dead. They put him in the boot of the car and Malone drove the car away and abandoned it. The vehicle belonged to Finn's brother and when he got his car back he found his dead brother in the boot. Finn died simply because he was a Catholic.

The gang, including Sevenstone, were charged with murder and were all sentenced to life imprisonment.

These interviews with Malone were the stepping-stone to a long and protracted campaign against forces of evil, by my colleagues and me. There was no let-up day-to- day from the coalface of terrorism.

These were the days when detectives had been stretched beyond belief with the interviews day in and day out interrogating prisoners for very serious offences relating to murder and terrorism. So, I suppose one could forgive some detectives who were working at the 'coal face' so to speak, from disengaging themselves from some of these interviews with these scumbags.

As I have already pointed out these terrorists had been schooled in the art of anti-interrogation techniques by their American 'friends' so maybe some detectives thought it was futile to talk to them and waste their time and breath. Some read newspapers or filled in their overtime sheets, that was always a good one but more often than not the crossword always passed quite a bit of the time especially when they got stuck on four down and maybe three across. As I was hopeless at crosswords the only thing left for me to do was to try and get some reaction from the prisoners so I used to tell them jokes.

During one such interview with a Republican prisoner who was involved in the attempted murders of security forces in an army Land Rover in the Anderson town road. He, with others, fired a rocket on a four vehicle patrol, luckily the device only hit the back wheel of one of the Land Rovers, saving numerous lives. Fortunately, no one was injured in this attack.

I tried quite a few jokes with this prisoner; his name was Seamus. Nothing seemed to work.

'By the way, did I tell you about Paddy and the two arseholes? no response there but I continued.

In a small village in Ireland the Garda Siochana (that's the Irish police) stopped Mick and Seamus who were walking down the street and told them that there had been a bad accident. The Garda thought that the person who had died in the accident was their mate Paddy who had been very badly burned and was not recognizable and could they identify him. Mick went in first, "Yes badly burned, badly burned, but you will have to turn him over." They turned the body over and Mick said "That's definitely not Paddy", "Why's that?" asked the Garda, "Cos Paddy's got two arseholes", replied Mick.

'Seamus then went in and said the same thing. "Definitely not Paddy, cos Paddy had two arseholes". The Garda then asked both of them "How come Paddy had two arseholes?"

'Well it's dead simple, we were always together the three of us, me, Seamus and Paddy and every time we walked down the street people used to say "Here comes Paddy with the two arseholes".'

This joke did it. Seamus, the prisoner, cracked up. He was wide open now, so much for the anti-interrogation courses. It also cracked up my colleague who was doing the bloody crossword.

Here was a, man who hadn't spoken for four days. He had been staring at the interview room floor and walls and counting the small holes in each tile on the walls.

He was about thirty years old, a member of the IRA, married with two young sons.

'By the way, just to let you know that if you have miscalculated the holes in the wall panels there are 32,327.1.' (The .1 was a dot from a ball point pen.)

Needless to say I did gain a rapport, of like, with this prisoner. Instead of gazing at the floor and tiles he now looked directly at me and every few seconds burst into laughter at the Paddy with the two arseholes joke. I knew then I was dealing with a fellow Ulster man who underneath it all had a sense of humour similar to that of my own.

I continued speaking with him, 'Why are you teaching your children to be like you? Full of hatred, hiding from the police and the Army and worrying when will the next time be, when the security forces come knocking down your door at five o'clock in the morning, frighten your family and drag you off to be interrogated again, not ever knowing if you will be home again. What sort of a life is that for them? You should be doing what normal fathers do, taking your boys on an aeroplane to Disneyworld and them asking you "Are we going to see Mickey Mouse daddy and Donald Duck?" Instead they are asking you "When are you coming back home daddy, will you be away a long time, this time?"

'What will happen if your sons marry a policeman's daughter, what will you tell him and also what will you tell your grandchildren?'

He was pensive, he didn't respond immediately but it was the first time I saw tears in his eyes...first laughter...now tears. I knew I had got through to him...the futility of terrorism!

I informed him shortly after this interview he was being released without charge. Maybe we hadn't been able to bring him before a court of law but I really did think I had got through to him in some way. The relief showed on his face and the tears rolled down his cheeks. He put his hand out towards me and we shook each other's hand.

I said, 'I hope you've learned something in here Seamus.'

He replied, 'Absolutely and thank you.'

'I never want to see you back in here again.'

'Don't worry you won't,' he said.

I often have wondered over the years if he and his sons ever caught that plane to America.

Chapter Twenty-Two

Dark Days

As time passed, even I could see a change in my colleagues and myself. People I knew to be loving, kind family men and women became agitated, aggressive, depressed human beings. Consumption of alcohol became the norm after long and hard interviews, which sometimes lasted several days. When success was achieved our authorities were quick to recognise the stress we were under and a bottle was placed on the table. Alcoholism within the RUC had reached a new depth. Stress and depression was blatantly obvious. I knew that one day something would have to give, and it was with great sadness and regret I learned of the suicide of one of my colleagues, Derek Cuthbert, who shot himself with his personal issue weapon on Christmas Day. He must have seen this as the only way out.

Suicide followed suicide. My friend Fergal Wright was another victim of the pressures that were placed upon ordinary men and women who had no training or counselling to deal with such depressing and violent situations. People looked upon us as being the hard core of the fight against terrorism at Castlereagh and Gough

Barracks (another holding centre in Armagh). Little did they know of the human cost that they were asking us to pay. A lot of my uniformed colleagues who were out on the streets of Northern Ireland paid for their dedication of duty with their lives and physical injuries that were inflicted. We were cocooned in our own world and our injuries couldn't always be seen. We were in constant mental torture. Time off with sickness was our only escape, as we had to get some respite from this way of life.

We lived with threats of murder to each and every one of us. Policemen were targeted and murdered in their own homes regularly. I was never without my gun as I also lived in fear. I could never relax, as I was always extremely aware of my surroundings and possible threats to my family and me. An evening at a restaurant was no different. I always had to sit facing the entrance and was constantly vigilant of who was present and who entered the restaurant. Driving home was also dangerous. I was always conscious of being followed and targeted. I never let my guard down and slept with my gun never more than an arm's length away.

A walk one early evening with my dog almost ended in tragedy. I had returned home from another hard interview and had my supper then took my dog Sam for a long walk. There was snow on the ground and it was just dusk when I started my walk. I walked for about three miles through the countryside near my home about fifteen miles from Belfast. It was now dark with only the moon to lighten up the sky. Sam started to growl and become agitated. My hand tightened on the handle of my gun and my finger moved onto the trigger. I felt as if I was being watched. From the hedgerows to my left I heard movement, then suddenly I heard voices in the darkness shouting, 'Get him, get him.' I brought my gun round in front of me. Sam was now barking at the hedgerows and I was met with a hail of snowballs and shrill of laughter. I could feel the hairs on the back of my neck standing up and a cold sweat broke out on my body. I was shaking with fear. I thought for a few seconds that I was going to die. It was only my two young sons, George and Keith, playing a joke on me. How normal for children to throw snowballs, but how tragic this might have been. It was unbearable to think about the consequences as I returned my gun to my coat pocket. I could have shot my boys; I was so full of fear.

I beat my sons and I screamed at them never to do anything like that again, but they were unaware of what might have happened and how close they had come to losing their lives. I made sure that night that it was me who put them to bed. I hugged them and cried while trying to explain my fears to them and trying to make them understand why I reacted as I did. This episode haunted me for some time. I often questioned why I had left the building trade. Nothing had prepared me for a life like this.

Since that incident I felt as if my relationships with my boys had changed. I no longer felt as close to them as before and I never discussed the situation with Anne. I kept my feelings to myself – what a price to pay.

Home life didn't seem to exist anymore and relationships were deteriorating. Even Sunday lunch with the family was interrupted by requests for me to return to work. It became clear to more senior officers that certain detectives gave the job more than 100% of themselves, and subsequently those detectives were the ones requested by other divisions to be in charge of the interviewing. My ability, it seemed, was well known.

'George, you don't have to do this job. You know you can always go back to the building trade,' Anne said to me. She could see how I had changed and how insular I had become. There was no time for Anne or the children now.

I was called out from home just as I was eating my Sunday lunch to interview a prisoner, we will call him Barry Little. This suspect had allegedly kicked down the kitchen door of a house in West Belfast and had shot a boy who had been involved in IRA activity. The police dogs had found him hiding in the bottom of the garden.

Little was a dark-haired fella, thin and about forty-six years old with dark grey to black eyes. He sat there and stared ahead of him for at least three days. I thought he would never speak to me. I tried all the ways I knew to get this perpetrator to admit his crime. He kept himself fit performing his daily exercises in his cell, and after each of my interviews he always did one hundred press-ups.

I had a feeling I was missing something with this guy and couldn't quite put my finger on what it was. Northern Ireland is a small place compared to the rest of the UK and no one had heard of Barry Little, which was unusual. All we knew was his name and that he spoke with an English accent.

I kept on with different lines of questioning; I would not give up. To my utter amazement he decided to speak to me. He probably realised I wasn't going to go away and that it was going to be easier to try and give me a little something of which I wanted. I spoke of his family and asked him why he was in Northern Ireland in the first place. His reply to this line of questioning was, 'I've already lost my family so I don't give a shit.'

After this sudden outburst he clammed up and again stared at me for another half-an-hour.

'How did you lose your family; did you kill them?' I continued.

'No, the Israelis did it for me,' he replied.

'Israelis in England?'

'No, West Bank, Gaza Strip.'

'Did you live there?'

'My wife and kids are Palestinian; the Israelis bombed a terrorist's house next door to us and killed all my family as well. Bullshit if you don't believe me!'

I did actually believe him, but still couldn't understand his connection with Northern Ireland, and he wasn't helping me where that was concerned. I'd obviously bored him enough with my questions in order for him to tell me about his family, so I thought: it's time to bore him some more!

I eventually found where he had been residing and arranged a detailed search of the flat in Antrim Road. I also was present during the search of the grubby one-bed flat with a small bathroom. We found nothing at first, just a few clothes, papers, magazines and several cigarette ends in the dirty ashtrays. I ventured further into the bathroom and began searching thoroughly. That's another thing we learnt at training school, how to search thoroughly, and so I did. In the bottom of an 'Old Spice' shaving stick I found a piece of paper and written on it was a telephone number.

It was the following Monday before Little finally spoke to me.

'There's more to you Barry than meets the eye, isn't that right?' I said. He continued to stare at me.

'These are dangerous people you're working for, especially when you're out murdering people. On whose behalf are you doing this?'

'Just my family,' he said.

'So, that's how you got to work for MI6 then, is it?'

'I'm not prepared to answer any questions until I speak with somebody.'

'I've got news for you Barry; I'm not letting you speak to anyone unless you speak to me first. Now, who are you working for?'

He agreed to speak to me; perhaps he didn't think I was such a bad fella after all. By now, after so many days, we seemed to have a rapport with each other and I suppose he felt he had to talk to somebody in order to relieve the situation one way or the other.

He was married to a Palestinian girl and they had two children. After the tragic accident he was approached by the Israeli Intelligence, Mosaid, to tout for them on the West Bank where he was employed for a number of years, but had to return to England when things became too hot. He was approached by MI6 whilst on a flight to the UK and was then brought in for questioning and asked if he was prepared to go to Northern Ireland.

His contact in Northern Ireland was a fella called Pat Meacher. Both men were given a safe house and were given a number of tasks by MI6, in exchange for immunity to prosecution. He was asked to kill a professor's wife and was paid five thousand pounds for the task. However, this task was abandoned and he was paid another five thousand pounds to keep him quiet. He didn't know why he had to kill her and never asked any questions.

'I'll kill anybody for money, whether it be a woman or not,' he told me.

'You know I'll never appear at court Geordie; you better tell your authorities about me. They will want to know about that piece of paper you found.'

I'd never told him I'd found the paper with the telephone number on it.

'What paper's that?' I queried.

'The paper you found in the bathroom. If you phone that number, I'll be out of here within twenty-four hours.'

'That's what you think; you're in Northern Ireland now, not England,' I snapped.

'Phone that number Geordie and you'll be relieved of having to do a big file.'

I laughed at that; it was certainly true he knew what he was talking about.

My district inspector, Billy King, telephoned and got straight through to MI6 Headquarters. 'Is this Pat Meacher's handler?' Billy asked. The phone went dead, but within the hour I was summoned to the detective chief inspector's office where I met with two senior officers from Special Branch.

I related my story to the officers. In turn they requested to see my note book and journal. They examined my notes and then asked me if I'd any more documentation. I told them those were the only notes I had, but they didn't believe me.

'Don't be smart with us Detective Douglas. If you've any more notes we wish to see them.'

'These are the only notes I've got,' I replied. I was puzzled.

'We are keeping these and you'll get them back when we're finished with them,' and that was it. They told me to terminate any interview I had with Meacher, but to also charge him with attempted murder. I couldn't understand the logic. I still hadn't finished interviewing him. No explanation was given to me, other than it was an internal security matter.

Meacher was taken to Musgrave Street police station, where he was lodged to await appearance before Belfast Crown Court on the following Monday morning. I received a telephone call on the Friday prior to the court appearance to tell me Little couldn't appear at court because he was ill. On the Monday morning I arrived at court and was informed that Little had died of a heart attack in police custody on the Sunday night. I thought it was a joke at first, but then I was told to collect his property and return it to his brother who was flying over from England. I was suspicious; this man seemed very fit, and how did they know it was a heart attack? There was no post mortem; in fact, that's the last I heard about the man. It was very strange as death in police custody is always of great concern and one would always expect an internal investigation into such matters. No such investigation here.

My authorities thought I knew more. I did know that Meacher too had disappeared off the face of the earth as well. He was nowhere to be found.

As a result of this case my telephone was tapped and my mail was interfered with. I believe Barry Little is still alive and is probably working for the authorities elsewhere. Little was right; he never appeared before the court.

I felt very let down by the authorities. I'd worked constantly these last couple of weeks interviewing Little for hours and hours and eventually, when I was making inroads, I was told to terminate my interviewing. All of this was to the detriment of my home life; I was beginning to become very disillusioned with the police service.

Chapter Twenty-Three

A Different Way of Life

I had been a detective for a number of years but had never attended the compulsory detective training course. These courses were of a ten-week duration and were held on the UK mainland. All officers from the RUC either attended the police college at Hendon or Bishopsgarth at Wakefield, Yorkshire.

My dear friend and colleague, Detective Inspector Billy King, decided I needed respite. He suggested I go on the course at Wakefield. My worry was the studying, as I couldn't even begin to think about it.

'You don't need to concern yourself about that George, it's just a PR exercise, there's no exam at the end of it,' Billy explained. I really didn't want to be away from the family for ten weeks, and I knew I would have to do the course at some stage in my career, but when I heard there would be no examination I decided maybe I did need the break and I would give it a go.

I went to Bishopsgarth hoping to learn something of the English method of policing, but in comparison, it was completely different to the implications of policing in Northern Ireland. None of the police establishments were surrounded with barbed wire fences nor were they guarded by sangers. A sanger, is a security look out post at the entrance to each police station. The police officers in England, Scotland and Wales were not in the habit of searching underneath and around their private motor vehicles for explosive devices prior to leaving their homes, as was our routine. As a rule, they would not carry personal firearms and there were never threats made towards their families, which was always a worry to us. Even a simple task such as hanging out uniform police shirts on the washing line could not be done in Northern Ireland, and the children of policemen could not tell their peers that their father was a police officer.

I arrived at Bishopsgarth on a Sunday evening in March 1983 with a colleague, and not a barbed wire fence in sight. Life was normal here. I asked our chauffeur if he was sure we had arrived at the police training college as it looked more like a country house.

My room was small but adequate with a bed, fitted wardrobe, a desk and a wash-hand basin. It was just like being a single man again.

We all met in the bar that first evening and introduced ourselves over a few drinks. There were four classes on the course with about twenty-five detectives in each class. Life might not be too bad here, I thought, as our time was our own after lectures and I had no worries about losing my gun or anybody shooting me and socialising and recreation seemed to be the order of the day.

We were informed by the commandant of the college the next morning that ours was the first course to undertake a final examination. I was horrified and thought it just my bloody luck. I planned to have this out with Billy King when I next saw him! I realised then that some studying would be necessary, much to my horror.

Each student introduced themselves to the class. When it came my turn I gave a little of my background and then said, 'I just want the instructors to understand that should I come last in this first ever final examination, I don't wish you to feel inferior about your teaching capabilities. It won't be your fault as I'm only here for the R & R.'

The class erupted with support. 'Go on George, you tell em,' they encouraged. I could see then we had a class with experience and of course a good sense of humour. We all understood one another.

The Roof Top Garden in Wakefield was apparently the place to go in the evenings. With the beer at ten pence a pint, it sounded good to me. 'That's a load of bollocks,' I said to my mate, another George. 'If it's ten pence a pint the place will be packed and you'll never get near the bar, but we'll go for a laugh. These Englishmen must think us Irishmen are stupid.'

The beer was only ten pence a pint and it was packed. Our feet were sticking to the carpet, just like some houses I'd been into in the process of daily policing. It was a lengthy wait at the bar to get served but one the lads managed to get ten pints for the ten of us 'techs' waiting in anticipation. Wonderful, I thought, as I stood looking over the balcony of the nightclub gazing at the flickering lights and the young people dancing on the dance floor. It had been a long time since I had done anything like this and I was enjoying my sense of freedom.

The relaxation was short lived. George and I hit the floor simultaneously as the deafening explosion erupted from below on the dance floor. Our arms covered our heads in protection, awaiting our next move. I looked up gingerly from underneath my arms and saw everyone else standing around me drinking their pints. They gazed down at George and I who were still lying spread-eagled on the ground. 'Come on you two, get up George, it's your round,' they joked. I wondered what had happened as I climbed to my feet. My relief came as I was told the loud explosion was the disco display featuring a *Star Wars* spectacular! We all laughed about the incident and I thought how kind it was of them all to make George and me feel so at home!

I'd spilt most of my first pint so I took charge of the kitty and waited my turn at the bar. I bought the next round and tipped the barman a fiver. From then on I only had to raise my hand and the beers appeared – no more waiting. My action seemed to have been noticed by a very attractive young lady standing by my side. 'How did you do that?' she asked. I looked at her and could see just how attractive she was. 'How did you get that drink so quickly?' she enquired.

'It's just the way I asked,' I replied jokingly. 'Let me get you a drink,' I offered.

'Thank you very much. If you can get one as quickly as that I'd be very grateful.' I bought her and her friend a couple of drinks and they were definitely impressed at the swiftness of the service. The two girls joined our company for the duration of the evening.

I learned her name was Tara. She was a bright girl and seemed full of fun. We had a good laugh and enjoyed the evening – something that was to be repeated several times in the future. The next day Tara telephoned the college. She invited me to meet her in the 'New York Bar' that evening. The bar wasn't far from the college and I met her as arranged in the company of the other lads. She was tall, well-made and had long blonde hair. She was about twenty-five. She had her own house and worked for a television company.

I was flattered by her attention. She had a very open and honest personality and I had the most fun with her I'd had in ages. The laughs were endless. For the first time in years I felt a sense of normality in my life. I was now relaxing big style and the pressures back home seemed a long way away.

During daylight hours we studied and at night we partied. It was hilarious to see heads nodding on desks during lectures and some fellas openly snoring. I don't know how I managed to keep awake. The first week seemed to me as if I'd been dropped into another world. Let's have more of this, I thought to myself.

Friday evening came far too soon and both George and I flew back to Northern Ireland and back to reality. My first port of call was the police station to sign out my personal issue firearm. Things at home hadn't changed. Family life carried on as normal – the kids had to be chauffeured here and there to their various activities and for the first time in quite a number of weeks my Sunday lunch was not disturbed.

I flew back to England on the Sunday evening and I was looking forward to being back. I saw Tara three times that following week and I knew my attraction to her was growing. She was such fun to be with and I felt totally relaxed in her company. We enjoyed dancing together and having the odd drink or two. Our interests were similar. It was all a long way from home and my responsibilities. I pushed these thoughts out of my mind, for those moments anyway.

I stayed at Wakefield one weekend and by chance happened to see Tara at another nightclub, Madison's. I was so pleased to see her and we had a very exciting and romantic evening. We danced long into the night to slow sultry songs by Barry White. We spent the rest of the weekend together and visited York City and the Yorkshire town of Howarth, the home of the Bronte family, on the Sunday. It was a lovely two days. We held hands on our walkabouts and Tara was very tactile and I enjoyed this closeness. I wanted so much to hold and kiss her as never before but I constantly held back thinking of my responsibilities to Anne.

'Douglas has pulled the best looking bird in Wakefield,' one of the lads said one evening when we were all together having a drink. I knew how I felt about Tara but I wouldn't let my side down as I knew I would get myself in deeper and deeper and it wasn't fair to her or my family. However, we still saw each other almost every evening.

Part of me was saying 'you shouldn't be doing this George' then the other part of me said 'you're a long time dead, enjoy it whilst you can'.

When I visited Tara's home we spent our time talking to each other. I shared my thoughts with her about the job and my family. I didn't keep anything back from her and I was completely honest about Anne and the kids. She told me how she had never met a fella like me before and couldn't understand why I wouldn't make love to her.

I kissed her long and passionately that evening. It was beautiful and I seemed to have waited so long to do it. God, did I want her then.

I pushed her away from me. I don't know how I controlled myself and I was desperately sad about what I was doing to her. She wanted me to make love to her but I couldn't. My feelings were growing stronger for her, but how could I live with myself. I knew it had to stop but we continued to see each other until the course ended, we had become very close.

The final evening was an emotional one. I met Tara after the final course dinner for what I thought would be the last time. We went to the 'Roof Top Gardens' where I had first met her. There was no beer at ten pence a pint so we both got pissed, Tara on Bacardi and Coke and me on Brandy. It was a difficult decision to make but I didn't go back to her house that night. Tara was a very desirable girl and I knew I would miss her.

To my surprise Tara was at the Airport when I was leaving the next day and she handed me a red rose and told me how much she loved me. I explained, as I held her in my arms that one day she would meet a fella who would look after her and maybe even have a family of her own – I couldn't offer her that as I had my own life. 'Where will I find him George, if ever?' she asked. I said my goodbyes with a heavy heart and very mixed emotions.

On my return home I couldn't look Anne in the face. She knew something wasn't right and I knew I had betrayed her trust. I returned to work the Monday morning with Tara foremost on my mind. Awaiting me on my desk lay a pink envelope and in it a very passionate letter from Tara. She told me again how much she loved me and wanted me. Letters arrived daily as did telephone calls. I was under pressure to return to England.

Foolishly, I made an excuse and told Anne there was to be a class reunion back in Wakefield. 'That's awful early to have a reunion,' were Anne's words. I don't think she believed me.

It had been three weeks since I had seen Tara and she met me at the airport. We went straight back to her house where she had a bottle of Champagne waiting for us. We went straight to bed. I held her close letting my feelings explode on her. I now felt free to love her as I had waited to do for so long. She knew what she wanted and was taking it while it was there. I willingly responded and lost myself in our embraces. Lovemaking had never been like that for me. Anne was my only other sexual partner and this was a new experience. With Anne and I it was always me who instigated lovemaking and although she wasn't a passionate woman I did love her.

That weekend I spent at Tara's house was wonderful and a time which I will cherish. All my stresses of life had drained away from me and I was able to push all thoughts of Northern Ireland, home life and Anne to the back of my mind until I returned home to Belfast on Sunday night.

However, feelings of guilt soon overpowered me. I was very quiet and Anne knew something was wrong. How difficult it was to cope with the guilt. During that week I had made my decision never to contact or see Tara again. It was the only way I knew how to handle the situation. Anne kept asking me what was wrong and I would always tell her there was nothing. 'Anne, I have something to tell you,' I said, when it eventually became too difficult to keep to myself. 'Come and sit down, we need to talk,' I said.

'What is it George, what's wrong?' Anne asked. She had looked unhappy for quite a while now and I knew she suspected something was not right.

'I've been seeing a girl in England called Tara,' I explained. I carried on to tell her that I had nothing to reproach myself for when I was attending the course and that it was on the weekend when I had gone back that things got out of hand.

'Why did you do it? Why did you go back?' she sobbed.

'I had to get her out of my system Anne, that's why I went back. I know I shouldn't have gone, but I couldn't help it.'

'Do you love her, George?'

'No, I love you,' I told Anne, and I did. It wasn't that I had stopped loving Anne. We both cried and held each other closely. It was the closest we had been for a long time.

'You let it all get out of hand, didn't you? You have now to put it behind you.' Anne was worried the girl might have been pregnant and I had never even considered this possibility.

Anne was a loyal wife and a good mother to all the children, always putting others first, but with the lifestyle I was leading there was no time for closeness between us. Anne found it difficult to share her feelings with me and she wasn't a tactile person, so in return I closed myself down. It wasn't her fault she felt like that. I think it was her upbringing during the early years when her mother left them. This placed a heavy responsibility on Anne, as she was the eldest of the four children.

The only conversations Anne and I had were about the children, as I was always thinking about my job, and when I wasn't I had a glass in one hand and was talking about it. I was working over a hundred hours a month overtime, so it is no wonder my marriage was falling apart at the seams.

After our talk, I gave Anne my word that I wouldn't be in touch with Tara again, and although the letters kept coming, I did not respond. Eventually she wrote to tell me she had met a nice fella and I did write back then to say how pleased I was she had found a special person.

Life at home was strained for a while and I felt I had let my family down, but not just that, I had let myself down and I didn't feel good about it. One day I sat my kids down and explained to them that their Mum and I had been having difficulties and I had gone and done something I now regretted. Maybe I was wrong to share it with them but it was something I had to do.

I wish I could tell you that normality returned to our household, but how could it as work was totally affecting my way of life. Anne and I did sort out our differences; she was very forgiving and told me not to punish myself any more, but the gaping hole remained between us when it came to a physical and loving relationship.

Chapter Twenty-Four

My Deep Respects and Devastation

Thoughts of Wakefield were in my mind but I threw myself into work and the normal sixteen-hour days and seven-day weeks. Life revolved around doing the job and being with my family.

I became a member of a fishing club which had been formed by some of the lads at Woodburn RUC Station, and on the occasional day off we would enjoy a day's fishing. Fishing and shooting were my passions and this was reflected in my collection of wild life paintings. It was always a good day out and the craic was good. We were like a band of brothers and the fishing was secondary. Even a day's fishing had its complications – not only did we have all our fishing rods, buckets, lug and rag worms with us but we also were armed with our personal issue firearm.

Louis Robinson, a dear colleague, was part of our fishing syndicate, but his passion for his sport ultimately lead to his death. Louis and a number of prison officers were invited to fish in the Republic of Ireland. He had invited me to join them but I couldn't because I had to work. On the way home Louis was brutally murdered. The minibus carrying the men was stopped by an IRA heavily armed active service unit. They boarded the bus and asked for Louis by name and demanded to know which one he was. One brave prison officer stood up and confronted them, 'I'm Louis Robinson' he told them. He looked similar to Louis, with a thick dark beard. They didn't believe him and forced him and Louis off the bus.

It was a horrendous killing, too brutal for me to describe. His body was found, hooded and lying on a back road in undergrowth just over the border in Northern Ireland. He had been shot and his body could not be recovered immediately as it was known that the IRA booby-trapped bodies and so procedures had to be adopted to prevent further loss of life.

There is no justice and no person was ever made accountable for his death. There was no public enquiry for poor Louis Robinson and no 'John Stevens Inquiry' into his death costing the taxpayer hundreds of thousands of pounds.

IRA suspects, when arrested, regularly complained of inhuman and degrading treatment from officers of the RUC. They always had at their disposal the support services such as doctors, solicitors and Amnesty International for their well-being, but where were these groups or bodies when Louis met his death? They were always quick to demand their rights, but where were his? I have often thought, when will we see a public or any kind of enquiry into Louis Robinson's murder? I doubt it very much. Two unarmed superintendents travelled to the Republic of Ireland to visit a Garda Siochana Station

(Republic of Ireland police). They were also ambushed by the IRA on their return to Northern Ireland at Dundalk and were murdered. I don't recall any public enquiry about them either.

The Republic of Ireland, however, issued an enquiry into collusion between the Garda Siochana and the IRA over the two superintendents who were murdered by the IRA, but it seems the British Government continued to bend over backwards to pacify these murdering Republican thugs, yet there is no justice whatsoever for the security forces whenever they have been murdered in the Republic of Ireland or just between the border areas.

If the Republic of Ireland ever expects us Northerners to be a part of the whole of Ireland, it's time we too had justice.

How ironic it was. Anne had returned to work and was Acting Sister at the outpatient's department of the Royal Victoria Hospital. Her nursing had no boundaries. She nursed both sides of the sectarian divide. Anne was nursing people who were trying to murder my colleagues and me when they were injured. What a world we live in!

Anne didn't drive, so after a few sessions of me trying to teach her, I thought it would be better left to the experts. She was very efficient at many things and could turn her hand to anything, but driving was not one of them. I would drive her to and from work most days, but then to my total amazement she passed her test, and at the first attempt I might add. I often telephoned the Royal when I arrived at work just to make sure she had made it without any accidents. She always did, surprisingly enough! She also had the last laugh as it was me who had the accidents and she never had one.

Our Dickie died very unexpectedly in 1992. He had just retired after a long and distinguished service as the Chief Fire Officer in Belfast. He had been given the Royal Humane Society Award for saving a young boy who was drowning in the River Lagan. He hated swimming I recall. It was our Dickie who had bought me my first ever suit, which I had ruined the first day I'd worn it. I always remained a smart fella and was nicknamed 'The Suit' by my colleagues. Terrorists also referred to me as 'Big Geordie the Suit', among other names of course!

Dickie never changed and remained outspoken until the day he died. He is a sad loss to me as he always guided me when I was in trouble and if it wasn't for our Dickie I wouldn't even own my own house, let alone build three others. I helped him in return and remember building him a fireplace and laughed to myself when he paid me with a dozen eggs, plus one extra for luck... Dear Dickie!

I was stationed at Castlereagh and it was an unusually quiet Friday evening so I came home early. Anne was at home alone and the house seemed quiet and calm. 'George, I want you to come and sit down with me, I've something to say to you.' She had been working and was still in her nurse's navy blue uniform dress. She sounded serious and urgent. I did as she asked and waited for her words in anticipation. 'I don't want you to worry about what I'm going to tell you,' she said. I felt my stomach sink and I felt sick. What was she going to say? 'I've had a small lump on my breast these last few days, George, and I've had it checked out,' she told me. I was hardly hearing her words. Please, let this not be true, I thought. She carried on to tell me she'd had a biopsy done by the Professor at the Cancer Unit of the hospital where she was Acting Sister at this time. 'He's examined me and taken a biopsy, the result has come back and its positive breast cancer George,' she explained.

My body went cold and I was completely numb and my legs shook. 'What are you telling me Anne?' I was sobbing by now.

'I'm telling you I've got breast cancer but that I've caught it early. My operation is on Monday; it's all been arranged.'

I was totally devastated and didn't fully understand everything she was telling me. I was in turmoil and could only think about what I would do without my Anne and how would we all carry on without her. I didn't handle this information very well and thoughts were racing through my mind of how I was being paid back for being disloyal to her. Anne kept reassuring me that she would be all right and was more worried about me than herself. That was the sort of person she was, always putting others first. It was only later I got to know that on the day she received the result of the biopsy she kept a commitment to give a lecture to student nurses on the subject of breast cancer. She would never let anyone down.

Anne was in the Ulster Clinic for her 49th birthday. The operation involved a partial mastectomy and the removal of the lymph glands underneath her arm. The operation went well and it appeared we had got the cancer in time. Anne kept reassuring me, but also preparing me for any future reoccurrence of the cancer. The kids took it well and we all supported each other. I prayed every day and went to church every Sunday to thank my lucky stars Anne was recovering well. Maybe we had beaten it? She had regular monthly checks and came home each time with great news that she was clear.

Anne returned to work and felt she could now reassure her patients with first-hand experience that news was not always bad and that life could continue and be fulfilling. Anne gave some of her patients our home telephone number to contact her any time should they feel the need to. I thanked God Anne was well again; I was a lucky man.

Chapter Twenty-Five

Belfast to Portrush

Anne's illness certainly brought things home to me and I was determined that I would do whatever I could do for the cancer charities and hospitals.

'Are you going over to the club for a pint George?' one of the lads in the office enquired.

'Ssh,' I replied, 'the boss will hear you.' Our wee club in the Stranmillis area was from then on known as the 'Ssh' Club. We have a lot to thank the club for; it was a place where we regained our sanity after a heavy day of interviewing. It was a bolt hold and a place where we could exchange thoughts, anxieties, fears and of course, the craic was always good. That's where I used to collect my repertoire of jokes and escape the realities of life. It's a good job the walls couldn't talk.

To many of my colleagues the 'Ssh' was a Samaritan, but to others it was their downfall, as a few turned to heavy drinking resulting in alcoholism and later death. But to me, although I drank quite heavily from time to time, I have managed to control it.

The bar room was small with no natural light, but it felt secure. Had the paramilitaries known that on occasions there were between twenty and thirty detectives all drinking merrily together, what a coup it would have been for them. They could have wiped out the whole of the Castlereagh detective crime squad in one go.

Standing with a Gin and Tonic in my hand, I overheard a conversation between two of the lads. They were arranging to meet the following morning, as there was to be a cycle race to Portrush for a cancer charity. Feeling slightly inebriated I bantered them 'any 'eejit' can do that. It's only eighty miles away.'

'I can laugh at you George, you couldn't cycle all that way – we've both trained for months for it,' the very thin one of the two replied. I told them I could do it with one leg tied to my bike. They then challenged me to put my money where my mouth was. What could I do? I hadn't realised the bloody race was the following morning and I'd never ridden a bike for twenty-five years. Our Jim had given me one of his old racing cycles from the 1950s, which hadn't seen the light of day for years. I had to 'pony-up', they called my bluff.

At 2.00am that morning I arrived home pissed and found my old cycling clothes, hat and gloves. Anne was lying awake, as was the norm when I was out. She wasn't best pleased with me. 'You will have a heart attack, for goodness sake. Have a bit of sense George. These are young men and you're in your forties.'

I told her not to be so stupid and to go to sleep, as I had to clean my bike. I sprayed the 1950s Claude Butler racing bike with oil and cleaned it up as best I could. I packed my car with clothes I would need for the following evening in Portrush, as I assumed there would be some sort of revelling afterwards, and a six-pack of Budweiser, which would come in handy on my journey. I went to bed and Anne was still annoyed and pleaded with me not to take on the £100 challenge. But my mind was made up and I was out of bed at six-thirty ready for the challenge.

I arrived at the police centre at Garnerville. All I could see were several flashy bikes; it looked like the 'Tour de France', they all looked so professional in their cycling gear. But not me – here I was dressed in football shorts, cycling shirt, 1950s leather cycling hat and cord cycling gloves which had all belonged to my brother. Armed with my six-pack I joined the professionals who couldn't believe what they were seeing.

My fellow competitors opened their isotonic water and ate bananas at the Waterfoot stop on the coast road. I unfolded my six-pack which had been carried by the support van and thirstily drank two cans, accompanied by laughter from the others. Waterfoot was about half way to Portrush and I came within the first fifteen. The next stop was Portrush and I don't know how I got there, but get there I did. My bum was aching as I had no padding in this area and the cycle saddle did not give any home comforts, believe me. Out of twenty men I was seventeenth and I partied that night until about 2.00am. It was worth the pain! The lads had an extra whip round for me so I actually made £200, the hardest money I've ever earned, but I did live to tell the tale!

Word travelled quickly that I'd been a professional cyclist; however, every muscle and bone from head to toe in my body was sore. I don't know how I made it to work on the Monday morning, but I had to, as at that time I was involved in a big murder trial. It was my first day giving evidence at the trial of Peter Doughty, who had been charged with the murder of two Catholics: John and Kathryn May, who were husband and wife. It was alleged the May's were informants who resided in the West Belfast area. They were kidnapped from their home and taken to different safe houses in West Belfast where they were each tortured to try to get them to confess.

Their suffering for decency reasons could not be described. The treatment they received at the hands of their fellow 'Irish Freedom Fighters' was more than appalling and against all human decency.

Doughty spoke with a half-educated Belfast accent. Doubts were expressed as to the extent he was involved. I believed he played a major role but the way he portrayed it was that he was just the driver of the black taxi, run by the IRA, which kept moving the May's between the different addresses.

'I'm doing a degree in psychology at Queen's University,' said the small thin individual with pointed features that you wouldn't have afforded a second glance if you'd passed him in the street.

His words did not faze me; I wasn't impressed. 'Oh sure, another stupid degree Mr Doughty. Well let me tell you about my degree. It's called a Castlereagh degree. This is how I earned mine - speaking to lying fucking toe-rags like you, acting as if butter wouldn't melt in their mouth. Now let me tell you this, whenever you come to get your degree and you're standing on the platform wearing your gown and mortarboard, remember one thing –I'll be there too with the May's two children. Whenever everybody stops applauding your achievements, I'll be telling them about your other achievements; about how you murdered these children's mother and father and how you took them from house to house, so that your Irish Freedom Fighters could abuse and degrade them.'

I was consumed with anger and hatred for this individual and was emotionally charged. Tears rolled down my face and I was sweating profusely. Water ran down my back drenching my shirt. Physically I controlled my emotions. Doughty was crying too, maybe my words had finally got through to this murdering bastard. He admitted his part in the murders to me during that interview. John May was shot in the head in front of his wife, and when Kathryn May tried to make a run for it from the black taxi cab she was shot in her back. She still had her hands tied behind her back. God bless you both.

The morning of the trial commenced. 'You're walking very funny this morning Detective Douglas,' remarked the judge's 'batman' (the judge's right-hand man) at Belfast Crown Court.

'You'd be walking funny too if you'd just cycled eighty odd miles to Portrush,' I added jovially. He asked me why I wanted to do a stupid thing like that. I enlightened him that I was raising money for the Ulster Cancer Foundation and explained about Anne's breast cancer.

'Didn't you train for it George?' he enquired.

'No, I opened my big mouth again when I'd had a few drinks and couldn't back out of the challenge.' He laughed and told me to rub Vaseline around my bits. I told him it would take more than Vaseline – 'I've got two large lumps under my arse,' I explained.

After about one and a half hour's cross-examination in the witness box, sitting down on a hard wooden triangular seat, the pain was indescribable. I looked at the judge and respectfully requested his Lordship to allow me to give further evidence standing. He looked at me in astonishment. 'You want to stand?' asked the judge.

'Yes please my Lord, I do,' I replied. My request had bewildered him and I could see he was dying to know why I wanted to stand. (Witnesses always sat down when giving evidence on the Crown Court in Northern Ireland, unlike England where evidence was given in a standing position unless otherwise requested.)

My request came after long protracted questions by the woman defence counsel. She too was mystified by the request. I had stopped her in full flow of her questioning. 'Yes, of course you may stand Detective Douglas if it makes you more comfortable,' the judge added. The defence counsel was certainly not happy with me as I had interrupted her line of questioning, but I had to speak out as the pain had become unbearable.

During the lunch break the judge enquired with his 'batman' as to why I needed to stand. 'It is a strange request. Detective Douglas must be suffering from haemorrhoids,' he remarked.

'No, My Lord,' the batman replied and continued to relate my story. After the lunch recess I was kindly offered a cushion to sit on but I did give the rest of my evidence standing with permission from the judge.

Cross-examination did continue, but only for a very short period of time. Defence respectfully requested a recess to consult her client. After one hour Doughty returned to court and pleaded guilty to manslaughter that was accepted by the Crown. I still believe Doughty played a major part in the May's murders however, more than he told the court.

Chapter Twenty-Six

Back Down To Earth

You would think by now I would have learned to keep my big mouth shut, but when I saw it in the *Daily Telegraph* that two little sisters from Lithuania were coming to London for a bone marrow transplant and that they didn't qualify for any charity or government support, I decided to arrange a sponsored swim in order to raise a bit of capital for their operations. I recruited fellow officers, Dick Clement, Alan McCormick, Sharon Scott and Roy Cairns. The venue was a twenty-five-metre pool at Palace Barracks Army Camp. Each man would do twenty-five lengths, any stroke.

I trained secretly every day before work. This time I wasn't going to get caught out. Swimming was my passion and I was good at it. I knew I could win. I only revealed a week before the competition that this would be no ordinary swim and that we were going to swim wearing full police uniform, excluding boots and hat. They went mad at me, but I had been training in all the gear as well so I knew I had an advantage.

Terry Brown, another dear friend from Castlereagh, was the starter and with the loud hailer strummed up support from spectators who had come to the pool to watch the action. Terry was giving it plenty of banter and the friendly rivalry added to the occasion. Terry knew what a modest person I was and smugly waited for 'the off'!

I sped through the water and I calculated that I was at least two lengths ahead of my next competitor. On my last length I knew I'd won with ease and as I touched the side everyone applauded me. Then I heard Terry saying 'No George – you're two lengths behind, keep swimming.' I was confused, but I didn't question him and kept swimming. I swam even faster although all my efforts were in vain as two others had finished before me. I waited for the last man to catch up with me and we came in together. We raised well over £500. I couldn't believe I had miscalculated the lengths and it was only afterwards the swimming pool attendant revealed Terry had made me do two extra lengths. Terry would tell you that if I'd won he would never have heard the last of it. He's probably right!

Terry did the same thing in a charity football match. I'd scored three goals but no way was Terry going to give me 'man of the match'. I think he's trying to tell me something.

Our R & R was sometimes spent across the water with the Manchester boys. It started off with just police officers from the Greater Manchester police, but as the years passed we made other friends and associates and we are still friends to this current day. They looked after us extremely well and collected money for the Disabled Police Officers Association, sometimes taking part in the RUC raft race that was held every year at Portrush. Other forces within the UK were also very supportive of the RUC and made rafts to compete in the fun race.

It was like the start at Le Mans! Each team picked up their homemade concoctions called rafts and ran like hell to the cold shallow waters of the Atlantic Ocean. We paddled like hell out around the markers and the lucky ones made it back to the shore. Most of the rafts capsized before reaching half way round the course but it was a great day and well-remembered by all who took part. It was a real family day out.

My son Keith and I returned from Manchester after a heavy weekend with the lads seeing Manchester United and Arsenal play on the Saturday. Keith and my eldest son George were both now police officers in the RUC. We arrived back at Belfast City Airport on the Sunday evening and were met by officers of Special Branch. I was instructed not to go home. They informed me I was being targeted by the Provisional IRA and I had to attend Glengormley police station to get instruction from the duty inspector.

When I reached the Station no-one knew anything about it, so I contacted the chief inspector at Newtownabbey who told me not to go home and I would get full details the next morning. I was angry and felt totally unsupported. I told the officer I was going home and signed out my personal weapon.

I was given more details the following day and reassured they didn't think the IRA knew where I lived, but were not totally sure. Security Branch placed me on the Protected Persons list and I had the choice of either moving out of the home I'd built and moving with the family into an Army camp, or the authorities having to secure my home appropriately. I told them to secure my home as I wasn't moving anywhere.

Anne had been having her thee-monthly check-ups for about two years now and results were good. I always attend the hospital with her, but on one occasion the news was not good. She had discovered a lump on her back. No time was wasted and the lump was removed but it was bad news. The cancer had penetrated her lungs and my worst nightmare had returned. Treatment resulted in the loss of her hair, but the news was still not good. Anne was told she had six months to live. It was a devastating blow to all the family. They even tried a new treatment that involved taking stem cells away and culturing them outside the body. This was pioneering treatment and Anne was the first patient in Northern Ireland to try it. Anne said she would give it a try as it might help others in the future.

She was bombarded with cocktails of drugs and my authorities were helpful to me as I spent a lot of my time by her hospital bed. Anne seemed to do quite well on the treatment and left hospital in May 1994. But it was short lived and by August things deteriorated rapidly. She collapsed at home in front of Ruth and Keith and we were to be told that the cancer had spread to her brain. Anne was unable to attend Ruth's graduation at

Newcastle University, an occasion she had been looking forward to.

Our home was being secured with alarms, sensors and bullet proof glass. Anne was very sick and had to be moved from room to room while the work was being carried out. Anne was aware of the threat but we played it down. I knew who I had to see!

I was going to see people I had known from when I was a boy. One of them was high in the Republican movement – we will call him Paddy. He was a well-respected Republican man. I arrived at his home in West Belfast on a Sunday evening unannounced. He knew me well and when he opened his front door the shock on his face was a sight to see. I was the last person he expected knocking at his door.

'What the fuck are you doing here Geordie? You'll get yourself killed,' he said. I walked into the house uninvited; I was raging and didn't care about the danger.

'I'll tell you what I'm here for Paddy, your fucking outfit has put a threat out on me, but what you don't know is that my Anne is dying and has been given only six months to live. Just fucking tell them this and let me look after my wife until she dies, then I'm fair game. But if they come looking for me and miss I will personally shoot you and your family.'

'Geordie, it's got nothing to do with me, I wouldn't do that to you and Anne.'

He was panicking but I wasn't finished yet, I was on system overload and I continued. 'And let me tell you this Paddy, if they miss they will find out what a fucking terrorist really is.' With those last words ringing in his ears I left.

The visit only took a few minutes and I didn't hang about. I jumped in the car and sped off to safer ground. My hands were sweating and my adrenalin was pumping. When I arrived home I poured myself a large Gin and Tonic and sat in a darkened room gathering my poise before speaking to Anne. She was in bed as these days she only got up for a few hours. She knew a lot about my work, but I kept the more sinister events away from her and the family. That was a separate world.

The following day I challenged Special Branch about the information they had relating to my security. I felt they were deliberately sketchy about the details and refused to give me the source of their information. They didn't know how I was to be assassinated but the IRA paramilitaries had details of the vehicle I was driving and apparently where I lived.

I just prayed that my visit to Paddy gave me the extra time I needed.

Chapter Twenty-Seven

Comeuppance

Work still encompassed me as I had another big trial waiting in the wings. One of the defendants was Billy Mathers, a ruthless individual I'd had dealings with in the past, but unfortunately I never got him convicted. 'You nearly got me that time Big Geordie,' Mathers spat out at me as he left Belfast Crown Court some months earlier. He was an ugly man with huge buck front teeth.

'You're right Billy, I nearly got you alright, but just remember one thing, one day I will get you and I'll get you for a good one. The next time I'll make sure you won't intimidate the witnesses.' He left the court a free man after being found not guilty of attempted murder of a young girl, Helen White.

He'd entered a pool room in East Belfast and held the young girl down on the ground with a gun to her back. She was a Protestant girl whose boyfriend was a Catholic. The case was withdrawn at the court because the witnesses had been threatened and therefore refused to give any evidence. Luck was on Mathers' side this time, but not for long.

I parked my car in Cregagh Street, just off the Woodstock Road in East Belfast. It was about 09.30 hours when I saw Billy Mathers and one of his sidekicks, Tommy Case, walking in my direction. Both men were leading figures in a Loyalist murder gang. They were carrying a paint brush and roller and a screwdriver and were about to enter number twenty-two Cregagh Street with a key which they had already placed in the lock of the door when I reached them. 'Going to do a bit of work boys; that will be a change for you two?'

'Do you think so, Big Geordie?' said Billy Mathers as he turned the key in the lock.

'That's a nice big car you got there; wouldn't it be a terrible shame if when you came back somebody had burnt it on you?' he threatened me.

'You're dead right Billy, it would be a terrible shame. Is this your house, Case?' I asked. There was a silence and neither replied to my question. 'It would be a worse shame Billy if you cunts were in the house sleeping one night and some naughty person came along and burnt you bastards to death. That would be a terrible shame too, wouldn't it?' Again there was silence as they stared at me and fumbled to get the door open. 'I reckon my car will be safe enough until I get back, don't you?'

Their attitude changed. 'Are you back working this area Geordie?' Case asked.

'Why do you want to know that; do you miss me?' I enquired with a wry smile.

'We thought you were up Anderson town,' Case continued.

'No boys, I'm coming back to work here, I believe you's were looking for me!' (Meaning their East Belfast terrorist unit). I left the street happy with the fact that both Case and Mathers would definitely not be fucking with my car. I had yet to realise the significance of this meeting with these two scumbags – I'll tell you why!

Adriane Mary Lynch, a 25-year-old Catholic girl who lived in the Lurgan area of Northern Ireland, was in the wrong place at the wrong time, enjoying a Saturday evening visiting the Glentoran Football Supporters Club in East Belfast. She was with one of the band members who were playing a 'gig' that evening. She was a quiet, unassuming girl and was the mother of two small children. She was not streetwise and was totally naïve about the implications of visiting a bar in a predominantly Loyalist area of Belfast.

Tommy Case and Billy Mathers were also at the club and befriended Adriane Mary Lynch. Case's girlfriend Marion Johnson was also in the club and she had just returned from England that day after having an abortion, and on the say so of her boyfriend she was to befriend Adriane Mary Lynch.

Case had been released from the Maze prison a few days earlier for being an active member of the Loyalist paramilitary outfit that call themselves the Ulster Freedom Fighters (UFF). He was paranoid when new faces appeared in the bar and ultimately formed the conclusion they were IRA members who had been detailed to 'spy' on him and his cronies. He questioned Adriane about the Lurgan area where she lived which had a large Catholic community, some of whom were IRA sympathisers. He mentioned several names to see if she knew any of them. These names were men and women who were known to be either members or had connections within the IRA. Adriane admitted knowing some of these people, but in fact she did not know them and probably had never even heard of them. The sad thing was these acknowledgements cost her her life.

Case and Mathers in their pathetic wisdom decided Adriane Mary Lynch was connected to the IRA and was sent to spy on them. They arranged to take her back to their house in Cregagh Street on the pretence there was to be a party at the end of the evening. It was Marion Johnson's task to befriend and accompany Adriane to the party. They partied and drank and Adriane placed her favourite tape, the theme from the film *Robin Hood*, into the cassette player. She chatted and drank oblivious to the plotting and skulduggery going on behind her back, and proudly showed off the photographs of her two children to Johnson that she always carried with her in her handbag.

Adriane was enticed up the stairs where she was interrogated by Case and Mathers. They gagged and beat her until she was dead and wrapped her little body in the bedroom carpet, dragged it down the stairs and bungled it into the boot of Case's car. They dumped her body on some waste ground off the Raven Hill Road. When she was found her head was almost severed from her body. They had hacked away at her throat with a kitchen knife, trying to detach her head.

I was detailed to interview the accused due to the similarities between this murder and the murder of another victim who had his throat cut with a dirty piece of tin. Case and Mathers were never convicted of this atrocity, but I believed they were present when it happened and were part of the same gang. One didn't have to be a genius to work this out as it was the method of operation of this Loyalist gang. I could link Case and Mathers to the address as I'd previously seen them enter with a key and also Case had signed for the electricity supply to the house. The house had been virtually stripped bare and all the rooms had been repainted, hence the decorating implements they had with them on our prior meeting.

It was most important to this enquiry that we connect Adriane Mary Lynch to these premises and the accused seemed to have covered their tracks well, but I felt there must be some evidence which we had missed. Our breakthrough came when one of our uniformed officers came across the tape Adriane had placed in the cassette player prior to her tortuous death on that fateful night. Adriane's fingerprint was found on the tape which was still in place. We had now found that vital piece of evidence to connect the two accused to Adriane's death.

I sat in front of Mathers in the seven feet by eight feet interview room, a place I was used to and a room he was also accustomed to. I didn't speak, but wrote down his name, address and date of birth on the paper in front of me. I didn't need to ask him for his personal details as I knew them verbatim.

'Right Billy, do you remember the last words you spoke to me?'
Silence.
'Let me remind you Billy, your last words to me were, "you nearly got me that time Big Geordie". That was for the shooting of a girl called Helen White. I told

you one day I'll get you for a good one. Well, this day has arrived Billy, you're fucked!'

I laboriously pursued the truth, trying painstakingly to extract some feeling of remorse from this murdering individual. I bombarded him with questions but each one was greeted with utter silence, as he stared ahead at the blank walls.

Each interview was the same. He continued to stare at the blank walls, never seemingly phased by my questions or the environment. He had been detained in custody for about five days and even I was getting weary going over the same questions with no replies from him.

Then, he changed. His gaze was not at the wall, but at me. Maybe I was starting to get to him. 'I can see you're worried, Billy. There's a lot of people not too happy with you. That was a bad murder of an innocent young girl, and for what? Before you leave here you're going to tell me exactly what your involvement was. I know by looking at you you're not happy about what you and your scumbag friends did to this poor girl. Marion Johnson ransacked the wee lassies bag, tore up the photographs of her children and smoked all her cigarettes, and all the while Adriane Smith was rolled up in the bedroom carpet, waiting to be dumped.'

It was the fifth day of Mathers' detention when he confessed to using a knife from the kitchen drawer to cut her throat. Being Billy Mathers to the end he tried to blame everyone but himself.

'You got me this time Big Geordie you bastard,' were his parting words.

'You're right there, Billy, I got you this time,' I replied wearily.

I was happy my long interviews had paid off so that I could put this murdering individual where he belonged, but it would never change the circumstances. A young innocent girl had lost her life for no reason and her children were left without a mother.

Marion Johnson was an evil bitch. She was abusive and kept trying to stop the interviews with the tactic of pulling out her own hair. She was Case's girlfriend and was about twenty years of age. 'You're not content with visiting London to kill your own baby, but you had to help your friends murder another human being,' was one of my statements to her in an interview. She admitted to the part she played, acting on the instructions of her boyfriend, Case.

They all appeared at Belfast Crown Court and were sentenced to life imprisonment. As Mathers departed from the dock his words rang in my ears, 'I believe your wife's dying, Big Geordie, but sure a good looking fella like you can always get another one and knock her up the builder.' (Belfast slang for getting a woman pregnant.)

'Billy, that's more than you will ever do. I did get you for a good one, didn't I? Your murdering days are over now.'

'You'd better have eyes in the back of your head Geordie, it'll not be long before I'm out.'

Sad to say, he was right. It wasn't too long before he was out of prison, under the so-called 'Good Friday Agreement', as were many other individuals. He was drinking in a bar in the Newtownards area of Northern Ireland when unfortunately for him he was gunned down and sent to where he belonged. Ironically, had he still been serving his sentence, he would still be alive. There is a great quotation, 'Those who live by the sword, die by the sword'. He certainly did that.

Chapter Twenty-Eight

A Cloud of Darkness

Mathers was correct. My wife Anne was now very ill and I had spent a long time by her bedside during the trial and was only called to court when it was time for me to give my evidence.

On 22 December 1994 Anne left hospital for the last time. There was nothing more anyone could do for her. She was in considerable pain and struggled to breathe. She had the aid of breathing apparatus but that was of little consolation. In the early hours of the next morning, Anne deteriorated yet again. I telephoned the doctor but he would not come out to her and told me there was nothing he could do.

Anne looked into my eyes, she had had enough and I could see that. I felt helpless. She couldn't cope with any more pain. I lay with her and held her in my arms until she slept. She never awoke. I stayed holding her close to me for I don't know how long. My heart was beating loudly; what would I do without her? The pain had gone from her face and she was now in peace. There would be an empty void in all our lives and I would miss her terribly.

We'd spoken about this hour and she told me I was her only worry. She knew the kids would be okay and would get on with their lives and so must I.

Anne died two days before Christmas. Our Christmases were spent at home each year with the kids and sometimes Anne's Dad and her Aunt Lila. Friends regularly dropped in to see us on Christmas Day, full of their Christmas cheer.

Anne spent her last Christmas at home with us. I made the dinner for all the family. It was a difficult time but Anne would have wanted me to continue the way we always did. 'Always a family time', she would say.

There were over one thousand mourners at the funeral, which was held at Templepatrick Parish Church on Boxing Day. She was a very popular person and well respected within the community. It was difficult for all of us, but the support of family and friends helped me enormously throughout the first few days of Anne's death. Then I suppose the inevitable happened. Things quietened down, people were gone as they went about their business and continued with their own lives. Ruth flew back to Bangkok where she was now working and Keith returned to his work. My elder son George and younger daughter Sarah had their own families to look after. The once busy house was now quiet. I had lots of time to reflect, as I still hadn't returned to work.

Meal times in our home were always noisy as you can imagine with four kids all trying to talk at once, but they were all away now and there was just me, my memories and consuming a meal for one.

Victor and Reta, my farming friends who lived close by, phoned every day and invited me to eat with them regularly, especially on Sundays, which could be a lonely time. I don't know what I would have done without dear Victor and Reta. I spent the New Year with them and their family. I reflected on each New Year I had spent with Anne and my family and the times when I was called into work. If I had my life over I would certainly have done things a little differently.

I became resentful of everything and everybody. If it hadn't been for Victor and Reta and my good friend Billy King, I don't know how I would have coped. They were the only people who gave me the support I craved. You see, being a Douglas you were expected to get on with your own life and not feel sorry for yourself.

It was my son Keith who suggested I needed a holiday. I had been reading that there was to be a wildlife exhibition in Las Vegas by the wildlife artist Eric Forlee, and thought this may be a good opportunity for me to get away. Keith also managed to get time off work to accompany me and was a great support on the holiday. I took the decision while I was in Las Vegas to extend my holiday to visit Ruth in Bangkok. She was suffering silently over her mum's death and I wanted to make sure she was coping all right, being such a long way from home.

During my trip I became ill. I'd picked up a virus, probably due to being at a low ebb. These things have a habit of creeping up on you when you least expect them. I felt so ill I thought it was going to be the end of me. With this in mind I wrote a letter to Keith, giving him full instructions of the procedure to take in the event of my death during the trip. I know this may sound a little dramatic, but I felt this could be a possibility.

It was a long journey via London's Heathrow airport and on to Bangkok. Keith continued on to Belfast and I remained in the airport drinking at the Oyster bar in the departure lounge and consumed copious amounts of wine and champagne. It did the trick; I slept all the way to Bangkok. I was still feeling pretty poorly on arrival, but I suppose the long journey had not helped.

It was good to see Ruth; she looked thinner and it was obvious she hadn't been eating properly, but now that I was around I would keep an eye on her.

I spent the next two days in bed and recovered slowly enough for Ruth and I to take a trip to Hua-Hin in South Thailand, where the sea was turquoise and the beaches white sand. It was beautiful and I lay by the shore feeling the heat massaging my body; it felt wonderful. This was paradise after the last few years of worry and heartache. Maybe things would get better. Anne used to tell me they would, but I doubted that.

'Dad, your ankles are looking very red,' Ruth interrupted my thoughts. 'You really ought to cover them up.' Sure enough, she was right and for the next two days I could hardly walk. My ankles had swollen up like red balloons; talk about sore. What else could happen; surely I must get a reprieve soon.

I remained in Bangkok for a couple of months until Ruth reminded me I must think about returning home. I responded defensively. 'Don't you want me here anymore, Ruth?'

'It's not that Dad, but since you've been here I can't fit into any of my clothes.'

She was right, of course, we'd both put on quite a bit of weight, so with this in mind I knew it was time for me to leave. I suppose I was putting off the inevitable, but I would go home and continue, as Anne would want me to.

Chapter Twenty-Nine

Glimmer of Light

I returned back to work at Castlereagh and all it had to offer; back to where I had left off, nothing had changed. The interviewing of terrorist suspects continued; there seemed to be one murder after another. I was drinking heavily and the 'Ssh club' profits, thanks to me and my colleagues were going through the roof.

My friend, Billy King, was still my detective inspector, and one day he made a suggestion to me. 'George, why don't you join our golfing society?'

'I can't play golf, Billy.'

'You don't need to be great, just as long as you can hit the ball we will give you a high handicap; you'll enjoy it. We are all off to Spain in May for a week; you're coming with us and that's that.'

Fait accompli, I agreed. As Billy shook his head from side to side, as he always did, with a huge grin across his face he said, 'Douglas, that's the first time you've ever done anything I've asked you to do.' I smiled; he was right.

I bought myself a set of second-hand golf clubs, and looking quite the professional joined Billy and the golfing party at the airport. It was now Spring 1995 and we were off to Espana, and hopefully the sun.

We played plenty of golf and had a lively week. It was a most interesting and fun place to be, even though I was seeing most of it through the bottom of a glass. My first evening was spent talking to the local 'women of the night'. I didn't realise at first who they were, but they were buying me drinks. When I did eventually find out their trade, I spent most of the evening trying to dissuade them from doing so. I kept thinking of my Ruth and Sarah; they were about the same age and I felt sorry for them and the life they were leading.

Billy Smartt, another member of our golfing party, approached me. 'There's a girl at the bar and she's a policewoman and has been working in Belfast; do you know her?' I didn't, but went to speak with her. We spent the remainder of the evening talking and dancing together. I learned she was also a detective in London's Metropolitan Police and was holidaying with two girlfriends. It was the final night of her holiday and I enjoyed her company. Her friend Lizzy was with her and the three of us had a good laugh together. I hadn't laughed like that for a good while.

I was drunk, but I did remember that she was kind and gentle; in fact, she reminded me of Anne in many ways. She made quite an impression on me. Very nice, I thought. As she walked out of the bar, she looked back at me and waved. I looked at the piece of paper with her telephone number written on it. Her name was Sue; I liked her, but I wouldn't see her again.

The week was spent playing golf, but the golf came a close second to the drinking. I was going to drown my sorrows. It helped being away from home and I had constant company, saving me from being alone with my thoughts. It was only when I was alone that my skies would cloud over.

The holiday was over and I once more returned to work. I was sent to work in the Greater Manchester area on the Robert Black Enquiry. He was a convicted child murderer and was currently serving a life sentence. My job, along with six other detectives from the UK forces, was to investigate child murders from our own police areas and find evidence to connect this killer to each of the murders.

I spent a few weeks working in England, but travelled home at the weekends. It was an opportunity to contact long lost friends, and so I did. I telephoned Sue, the girl I'd met in Spain, and we arranged to meet in London. I hoped I would remember what she looked like. I knew I'd had a few drinks when we'd originally met, but surely I would remember her. These thoughts kept going through my mind as I looked around the bar room at London's Forum Hotel in the Brompton Road.

There they were, Sue and Lizzy, sitting under the mirror at the rear of the crowded bar, bottle of champagne and three glasses on the table. Start as we mean to go on, I thought, and we did! It was great to see them once again; I don't know where the time went, we all had so much to talk about and the champagne was flowing as if it was on tap.

The three of us ate in London's China Town. It was a good meal and the company was second to none. I said my goodbyes and put the two girls in a black cab and sent them off to Epsom in Surrey, where they both lived. I walked back to the Park International Hotel where I was staying, much the worse for wear, but deep in thought.

I kept in touch with the girls and visited them in London on a couple of occasions. Sue and I spoke on the phone frequently; then the calls became daily, then several times a day. We learned a lot about each other and we were becoming very close, but it was difficult to meet with Sue working in London and me in Belfast. On the odd occasion we met in London when I visited the art galleries; I was still an avid collector of fine art. We were growing fonder of one another and I could relax with her; we seemed to have so much in common. We were both detectives and had the same sense of humour. I could talk to her about my life with Anne and her tragic death. She empathised; she had lost her mother some years earlier to the same dreadful disease.

I needed to spend more time with Sue; the infrequent meetings were just not enough, but it was impossible. I'd known from the start that Sue was married, and what made it worse her husband was another police officer. It was a most difficult and upsetting situation. I felt wretched about that; I knew it was wrong and so did Sue, but we had fallen in love.

I was confused. I felt fulfilled with Sue in my life, but it was far too soon after losing Anne. I shouldn't be having feelings like this for another woman so soon after Anne's death. How would the kids react? It would never work out so I had to let Sue go. We couldn't be deceitful any more. We both knew it was right, to prevent anyone else getting hurt.

I was still working in Manchester; it was the final week of the investigation. Sue dropped the bombshell – she had told her husband of our love affair and that she wanted to be with me. My feelings were mixed, these were difficult times and far too soon to give Sue any commitment. I knew I had fallen in love with her, but at what expense, and to whom? I blamed myself for the turmoil in our lives, but I could not let go.

We managed to see one another more often, both in London and Northern Ireland. Sue stayed in my home, but always had her own bedroom. I introduced her to the family and I couldn't have asked them to be more supportive. They were all great with both of us and I think they were pleased for me, although we hadn't told them that Sue was married.

My thoughts remained private, even from Sue. There were bad days and it was sometimes difficult for her to understand the need to shut myself away and reflect. Sue helped me through the hard times and I know I couldn't have done it without her.

After many air miles, and much commuting, Sue retired from her job and came to live with me at the home I had shared with Anne, behind the bulletproof glass and sensors. Her life took on a new dimension. I don't think she expected the first two years of her retirement to be exactly as they were. Welcome to Northern Ireland!

It was routine for all the family, and now for Sue, who had to constantly be aware of her environment, checking underneath her car for incendiary devices prior to every journey, and making sure she wasn't followed home. I warned her never to reveal personal details to anyone she did not know. It was difficult enough for someone who was so open. It was a hard task retiring to a place like Northern Ireland and everything it had to offer, and I certainly was not the easiest person to live with. Sue coped with my deep depressions and anger quite well. They were frequent in the first years of our relationship; if that didn't put her off, nothing would.

Sue's personality was different to Anne's. She could be quick tempered when she felt wronged, and this often led to disagreements and hostility between us, but that was part of getting to know one another and learning how to live with another person and adjust to a new way of life.

Throughout the years of Sue and I being together, I've learnt to be far more tolerant, and I suppose Sue now knows how to handle me much better that she did in the early days.

Many who met Sue remarked on the uncanny resemblance she had to Anne, although she was a few years Anne's junior. Bob was still alive and his jaw dropped when he first saw Sue because of the likeness to his daughter. Bob and Sue got on well, which was of great comfort to me. Sadly, Bob passed away in the April of 1999, just prior to his eighty-fourth birthday.

Chapter Thirty

Retirement

I retired from The Royal Ulster Constabulary in 1996. I had served twenty-five years and I knew I wasn't well. Stress-related symptoms creep up on one slowly and are hard to recognise.

I have great bitterness towards the authorities, as I feel I was not diligently supported. My retirement on ill-health grounds was not even recognised by an Injury on Duty Pension. I was also deeply upset at not receiving my Long Service and Good Conduct Medal, a medal presented to all police officers in the UK when they have served twenty-two-and-a-half years' service.

I had served a total of twenty-five years, which included my five years' service in the part-time reserve. I was told my part-time service did not qualify. Shame on them; I am proud of my part-time service and proud of my colleagues, who gave their lives in the part-time reserves. To say that the part-time service did not count is a disgrace. My colleagues and I gave it our all, and more.

The perpetrators I put behind bars are all released now. I feel the powers that be, capitulated to the IRA and Loyalist paramilitaries and released the many murderers I'd personally convicted under the so-called Good Friday Agreement, and that is hard to take.

In defiance of this, in November 1999, after attending the Remembrance Parade in Whitehall, Sue and I went to Number 10 Downing Street. The purpose of my visit was to hand in my police medal in disgust at how these violent criminals were allowed to walk free, and not serve their sentences. What about the poor victims of these crimes; where was their reprieve? An officer of the Diplomatic Protection Service at New Scotland Yard informed me that I must hand in my medal at the gates of Downing Street and not at the front door. This appalled me. It seemed ironic that I was being refused this request, but yet the Prime Minister was inviting terrorists, some of whom I have interviewed, through the front door of 10 Downing Street, and wining and dining them. Where is the logic in that?

What is the difference between a terrorist who plants a bomb in Israel killing innocent people, and the terrorist who plants a bomb in Omagh, also killing innocent people? There must be something wrong; this is not just about terrorism in Northern Ireland, it's about terrorism all over the world. The message given is, if they bomb and kill enough people the governments around the world will capitulate to them. Need I say more?

Needless to say, I was escorted to the front door and was allowed to hand in my medal in protest. The officer asked me if I had anything else to add to the letter I had previously written. He said, 'I read all the letters that come into our office George, and your letter comes from the heart and not from the bile duct. Do you mind if I attach your letter to your medal?'

My final thought was: I feel I have just wasted twenty-five years of my life for nothing.

To this day, I have yet to receive an acknowledgement or receipt for my medal. I was however to learn that Her Majesty the Queen, at the behest of the British Government, was to award the men and women of The Royal Ulster Constabulary the George Cross. One day history will prove that for thirty years or more men and women of the RUC stood alone at the coal face in the fight against terrorism, only to have their names removed from history, and the plaques of the brave officers who lost their lives removed from police stations in Northern Ireland.

This was the price for so-called peace. A high price to pay!

*Wee Geordie handing back his RUC Medal at No 10
Downing Street Monday 12 November 1999 after
attending the Remembrance Day Parade at the
Cenotaph on 11 November 1999*

Chapter Thirty-One

A New Life

Sue and I, now both retired from the 'job', enjoyed spending our time together. Our hobbies included the garden, walking and now having the time to pursue other interests.

When Anne was alive I had started building again, purely for the family, constructing a small cottage at the bottom of our one-acre garden. However, I had lost all interest when Anne became ill and it was Sue who suggested we take on the task of completing it together. This we did, and Sue laboured mixing mortar by hand, and I built blocks and bricks. We were a good team and this helped me a lot with my recuperation.

However, I could not tolerate that the newly formed Northern Ireland Assembly included persons from both sides of the sectarian divide whom I'd previously dealt with at Castlereagh. I knew I had to get out.

My family and I had many holidays in Scotland where I pursued country sports, such as pheasant and grouse shooting in the Highlands. Anne and I had often talked about retiring there and running a wee coffee shop. Alas, Anne could never fulfil her dream.

However, Sue and I did leave Northern Ireland; it was really a matter of having to. I couldn't lead a normal life and was constantly looking over my shoulder. I'd had enough of that.

We made our home at the beautiful Dalriach House twixt two mountains of grandeur, Ben Chuialch and Schiehallion in the Tummel Valley. Sue took in the occasional guests for bed and breakfast, and I tended the seven acres of garden. The house, built in the 1800s in Tudor style, was a former hunting and shooting lodge, with huge rooms and high ceilings, and plenty of space for all who visited. The Douglas firs surrounding our beautiful home encompassed us with splendour, as did the roar of the Tummel River that flowed in front of the house.

The fine summers were spent swimming from our small jetty, which I repaired after many years of neglect and raging torrents of water that had passed over her throughout the years. We fished the river from our small 1920s clinker-built rowing boat. We never caught the salmon we always dreamed of catching, but trout and pike were in abundance, especially the pike, which always seemed to jump on the end of Sue's hook. Of course I never heard the last of that! Two of my grandsons, Bradley and Jordan, would say, 'Don't you think we should take Granny Sue fishing with us, Granda? She always catches the fish.' The pike tasted good, the river was very clean so it would be a shame not to enjoy the fresh fish. We cooked the fish with plenty of butter, white wine and herbs in the roasting oven of the Aga; they made a tasty meal for little hungry fishermen and grandparents alike.

I have five grandchildren, four boys and a girl. Karl and Curt are the sons of my eldest son George and his wife Lorna, and Bradley, Jordan and their sister Zara are the children of my youngest daughter Sarah. They all still live in Northern Ireland. I was sad to have to leave my family; I still miss them, but we are contented with the fact they can visit me and enjoy life in Scotland. Dalriach House was a splendid place for them to visit, with the seven acres of gardens for them to play and get lost in.

Ice and snow came and went; each season had its own beauty. Friends and family alike enjoyed our new piece of paradise, especially at Christmas and New Year, when the house was aglow with lights, decorations of gold and silver cones, which had fallen from the firs and collected from the garden by the children, Sue and myself.

Our dear friends Lizzy and Mark Williams were married in our home on a lovely late August day – Dalriach's first ever wedding. The groom and his pals enjoyed a swim in the river, prior to the ceremony! A piper played in the gardens and a harpist greeted guests as they took their seats for the ceremony in the drawing room that was beautifully decorated with flowers from the gardens. Sue and I were proud to be the witnesses on this special day.

I married my Sue on the 18th of March 2000 at the little Kirk in Kinloch Rannoch. It was a glorious crisp sunny day; not a cloud in the sky. Sue looked splendid in a specially designed tartan ensemble, with fresh flowers in her hair, and I wore a Douglas tartan kilt. We were surrounded by our family and dearest friends, and here's to you all – George, Lorna, Keith, Ruth, Sarah, Lizzy, Mark, Elizabeth, Rachael, Sam, Mike and Mary, Billy and Linda, Victor and Reta, Ivan and Jan, Georgina and Ronnie, Brian and Susan, Stevie and Becky, Simon and Roz, Robert and Helen! And absent friends Terry and Roberta Brown.

Life at Dalriach would not have been possible but for the financial support and encouragement of my dear cousin and her husband Mike and Mary Newham; it would have been only a dream. They were our staunch supporters and we are eternally indebted to both of them.

My life was not all bad, you know, but the rest is another story, and I'm still here!

Dalriach House Tummel Bridge Perthshire Scotland